THE KENNEDY ASSASSINATION

DID OSWALD ACT ALONE?

Michael J. Deeb and
Robert Lockwood Mills

THE KENNEDY ASSASSINATION

DID OSWALD ACT ALONE?

Addison & Highsmith

Addison & Highsmith Publishers

Las Vegas ◊ Chicago ◊ Palm Beach

Published in the United States of America by
Histria Books
7181 N. Hualapai Way, Ste. 130-86
Las Vegas, NV 89166 USA
HistriaBooks.com

Addison & Highsmith is an imprint of Histria Books. Titles published under the imprints of Histria Books are distributed worldwide.

Library of Congress Control Number: 2023939521

ISBN 978-1-59211-344-6 (hardcover)
ISBN 978-1-59211-352-1 (eBook)

"It has been confirmed by our reporter in Dallas that President Kennedy is dead."

— Walter Cronkite, CBS News
November 22, 1963

Marilyn Burke stormed through the back door. Her Silver Spring, Maryland, home had been part of a subdivision built in the late 1920s. It was a working-class neighborhood then and still was.

The homes on her street were described as brick-to-the-belt, two-story structures. There were two bedrooms on the first floor. The previous owners had put in a bedroom, bath, and sitting room on the second floor for one of their parents.

Marilyn was a five-foot-four, one-hundred-fifteen-pound brunette. She was a very pretty woman and still slender after three children. She and her husband, Michael, used the second-floor sitting room for their bedroom, and their children slept in what had been the second-floor bedroom.

"Michael!" Marilyn shouted. "Have you heard the news?"

She had been to the local pharmacy. The doctor had called in a prescription for her three-year-old daughter, Ann. Her husband had not felt well either that morning and had stayed home, too.

She rushed to the front of their house. She expected to find him napping on the couch. He was.

"Michael, wake up."

He rolled over, feet on the floor, suddenly wide awake.

"Is something wrong with Ann?"

"No!" she gasped. "It's President Kennedy. He's been shot."

"Oh, my God! Quick, turn on the TV!"

They rushed into the small room at the back of the house, where they had their television set. They turned it on and sat on the couch holding hands waiting for the set to warm up and the picture to appear.

The image of Walter Cronkite came on the screen.

"President Kennedy died today at one PM Eastern Standard Time.," Cronkite announced. "His limousine was traveling from Dallas's Love Airport to a lunch meeting at the Trade Mart building when he was shot. He was rushed to Parkland Hospital, where doctors pronounced him dead at approximately one p.m. A twenty-five-year-old white male has been arrested by Dallas police. We will keep you informed as more information becomes available."

An image of President Kennedy appeared on their black and white television screen. The screen showed him emerging from Air Force One in Dallas, Texas, earlier in the day. Right behind him was his wife, Jacqueline. He gave the cheering crowd that great smile of his, waved, and led his wife down the airplane ramp.

Mike and his wife slumped back on the couch, and Marilyn gripped his arm. She began to cry.

"Oh, my God, Michael! How could this happen?"

Before he could respond, Mike had to gather himself. Tears were streaming down his cheeks, too.

Michael Burke was a Congressional staffer. He had worked for the House Committee on the Judiciary for the last five years. Like many men of Irish heritage, he had blue eyes and hair that was sort of rust-colored. A good six feet tall, he and his wife made a handsome couple.

"I don't know, sweetheart," he said. "But I do know, with Johnson in charge now, the military will have its way in Vietnam."

"You don't think he'd have had anything to do with this, do you?"

"We'll probably never know."

Then they both became silent and focused on the television screen.

THE FEDERAL BUREAU OF INVESTIGATION - MAY 1967

Helen Gandy answered the intercom that connected her desk to that of the director, J. Edgar Hoover. She had been his personal secretary for over a decade.

"Yes, sir."

"Mrs. Gandy, please have Bill Sullivan come to my office immediately."

"Right away, sir."

Bill was a Notre Dame Law School grad. He'd been with the Bureau since graduation and had become an assistant director with over twenty years of service.

After receiving the call from Helen Gandy, he immediately rose and went down the hall to her office. The walls were covered with plaques, framed honorary degrees, and other awards given to Mr. Hoover.

"You can go right in, Mr. Sullivan," she said.

He was struck by its Spartan plainness whenever he entered Mr. Hoover's office. He smiled at the shabby couch sitting against the dark paneling of the walls.

The director's desk had been placed on an elevated platform so that visitors using the wooden chairs in front had to look up when talking with Hoover. The walls were barren as well; not one photograph. The only adornment was two American flags flanking his desk and an FBI seal on the wall behind it.

Sullivan stood in front of his boss's desk.

"Have a seat, Bill."

"Yes, sir."

"This memo you sent me today."

"Is that the one about the House Committee on the Judiciary's plan to look into the Warren Commission's report on the Kennedy assassination?"

"That's the one," Hoover replied. "What do you make of it?"

"I think they're serious. With the off-year election coming up, I believe they want to respond to Mark Lane's book and the latest Harris – Washington Post poll about the Warren Commission's report.

"That poll shows that the number of Americans who now believe there was a cover-up has reached 45%. In fact, I think the same poll reveals that over 60% of the public believes there was more than one shooter. So the Judiciary Committee members want to be seen as responding to these suspicions."

"You think they're on to something specific about the commission's report?" Hoover asked his long-time deputy.

"Not at all, sir," Sullivan replied. "My contacts on the committee told me that there is nothing behind the move except public relations. The committee members are primarily concerned with winning their next election."

"That sounds innocent enough. But we went through hell with the Warren Commission. The rumor mill back then was vicious. I don't want this investigation to get out of hand. You understand me, Bill?"

"Yes, sir. May I make a suggestion?"

"Of course."

"The committee has staffers friendly to the Bureau. In fact, one staff member worked for me several years ago. We hired Mike Burke right out of Boston College; he majored in accounting. He turned out to be a good investigator for us."

"How long was he with us?"

"He graduated in 1957 from BC and stayed with us for a little over three years."

"Why did he leave?"

"It appeared to be the money. But I think his wife was nervous about him working for the Bureau. She wanted to live near her parents in Maryland and feared we'd assign Mike to some office out of this area."

"Can you control him?"

"I believe so, sir. I remember Mike was a good investigator, very thorough. But he wasn't stupid. Neither was he exactly an angel, off duty."

"Enough so that it would be a problem for him if revealed?" Hoover asked.

"He has three little girls now and a comfortable life. So I don't think we'll have a problem working with him."

Then Hoover asked, "The last I heard, John Conyers of Michigan chairs the Judiciary Committee, and Gerry Ford of Michigan is the Minority Leader. Is that still the case?"

"Yes, sir."

"Ford is a longtime friend of the Bureau; no problem there. Besides, he was a member of the Warren Commission. I'm sure he wouldn't want a lot of dirt dug up.

"I don't know this Conyers fella much, though. Best have Helen give me our private file on him. And, give me half an hour with Burke's file. Then get Gerry Ford on the phone for me. I'll see what can be arranged."

"Yes, sir."

SILVER SPRING, MARYLAND – JUNE 1967

It was almost eight o'clock on a balmy June morning. Mike and Marilyn were being lazy this Saturday, having their coffee and reading the Washington Post in bed. Their three girls were awake but were playing school in the adjacent room with the door closed.

"Listen to the girls, Mike," Marilyn said. Her children were playing school. Their eldest daughter Susan was the teacher. Her two sisters, Ann and Jackie, were the students. Susan was giving instructions to her two pupils.

They could hear Ann protest. "Why are you always the teacher? I go to school now, too."

Quick to pick up on a revolt in the making, Susan suggested. "You can be my assistant teacher today, all right?"

Both parents smiled. "Susan was quick to solve that problem, wasn't she?" Mike told his wife.

Marilyn smiled. "For now, maybe. But I'll wager Ann will be the head teacher before long," she predicted.

"You're probably right," Mike agreed. "Ann doesn't back off easily. Reminds me of her mother."

"A very admirable trait, don't you think?" Marilyn smirked.

Mike had finished catching up on sports and reading the editorial page. He turned toward his wife and put his hand on her leg under her nightgown.

"Neither does her father," Mike whispered.

"Oh? Is he after something, too?"

Mike slid his hand up his wife's bare leg until it could go no further. There she was warm to his touch. He began to move his fingers.

"Ohhh my. That feels good, Michael." Marilyn let the paper she was reading slide to the floor as she turned toward her husband.

They kissed as his fingers began to explore her more deeply. Marilyn pressed closer and opened her lips to his exploration, too. At the same time, she moved her hips in a slow rhythm, squeezing his fingers.

Just as she began to feel her muscles tremble, the door to the children's room slammed open.

Their youngest daughter, Jackie, ran out of the makeshift classroom and into her parents' bedroom, shouting.

"I don't care if you are the teacher!" she exclaimed. "I don't want to play school anymore; I don't like having two teachers."

She looked at her parents lying close together in their bed.

"Can we go outside yet?"

Marilyn had pulled the sheet up to her chin with a heavy sigh. Her cheeks were still flushed.

Mike fell back on the bed with a heavy sigh.

Lord. It never fails, he thought.

Marilyn slid out of bed and hurried into the children's adjoining bedroom.

"Come on, children," she commanded. "It's time to get dressed. Besides, we all need some breakfast; you too, Dad."

Jackie jumped on her parents' bed and climbed on top of her father. She moved her face close to his.

"Come on, Dad," she whispered. "It's time to get up."

Mike put his arms around his daughter and looked at her, eyeball to eyeball. "Why?" he said.

"Because."

"Because why?" he teased.

She began to giggle. "Because it's Saturday, and the sun is shining. That's why."

Mike rolled her over and leaned close. "When did you get so smart, little lady?"

Just then, Marilyn threw some clothes at them.

"You can get your daughter dressed if you please. We've wasted enough of this beautiful day in bed. Rise an' shine, you two."

Mike looked down at his youngest,

The last time your mother and I wasted a morning in bed, you were conceived, my little girl. Not a bad use of that beautiful day, I'd say.

***

Later that morning, everyone was out in the backyard picking up the debris from a recent rainstorm. Small branches littered the lawn. Marilyn wanted to plant some annuals in the flower beds today, too.

"What time did you get home last night? I gave up around ten and went to bed."

"I didn't get home till almost eleven. I hope I didn't wake you."

"No, you didn't. But what was that all about? I would have thought such big shots as Ford and your committee chairman, Conyers, would have more important people to meet with than one of their staffers."

"I'm sure you're right. But Chairman Conyers and Congressman Ford wanted to talk with me about an assignment. So they suggested dinner in town, at the Army-Navy Club. I could hardly turn them down."

"I understand that. You went to a fancy restaurant, too. So what did they want?"

"They want me to head up a review for the Judiciary Committee of the Warren Commission Report on the Kennedy Assassination."

"Holy shit, Michael!" Marilyn exclaimed. "That sounds pretty heavy. That report, if I remember correctly, came out sometime in 1964, didn't it?"

"That's right. September of that year, I think."

"Didn't it answer most questions about the assassination?"

"Apparently not, sweetheart."

"So just out of the blue, these two big shots decided to muck around and stir up that horrible event?"

"That's about the size of it. With midterm elections coming up, they want to be seen responding to an increasingly skeptical public. The entire Warren Commission study rests on the assertion that one shooter killed President Kennedy and wounded Governor Connally. But recent polling data shows a growing belief that there was more than one shooter."

"And they want Michael Burke to check it out, right?"

"You got it, sweetheart."

"No, I don't 'got' it, Michael. Why did they choose you?"

"It could be my charm. But it appears that my record as an investigator with the FBI and the fact that the bigwigs at both the Bureau and those on the committee trust me was important in their selection."

"Excuse me if I seem skeptical, dear. I certainly don't doubt your skills or underestimate your character traits. And I'm thrilled they are being recognized. But you know I don't trust those FBI people. That's why I urged you to leave the Bureau years ago. How did people at the Bureau even become involved in the selection?"

"My old boss at the Bureau, Bill Sullivan, got wind of the proposed investigation and talked about it with his boss, Mr. Hoover. Somehow, in that conversation, Bill recommended that Hoover suggest my name to Conyers and Ford. He did, and they agreed; simple as that."

"Oh, come on, Michael. You know them better than that," Marilyn insisted. She faced her husband, angry now, with hands on her hips.

"Nothing is simple with that bunch at the Bureau. They're never looking for the truth, but they're always looking to protect their butts."

Mike's wife seemed to be warming to the issue.

"Does your old boss Sullivan feel that the Bureau is safe with his former employee in charge of this investigation? "

Holy crap! What an interrogator she would make.

Mike was getting hot, too. "Marilyn, I don't have any idea what Sullivan feels. What I do know is that I intend to conduct a thorough investigation and afterward provide the Judiciary Committee with an honest report. OK?

"Come on, sweetheart. Let's get back to the children and finish this conversation later. All right?" Mike asked.

"At least you're right about one thing. Michael. We should get back to spending time today with the kids. It makes me angry all over again to think I've allowed us to waste even ten minutes talking about that rotten bunch at the Bureau."

Whew! When Marilyn hates, she goes all the way."

THE FEDERAL BUREAU OF INVESTIGATION

Hoover was beginning his week with the usual morning meeting with his deputies.

"Bill," he addressed Bill Sullivan. "How did it go with the Judiciary Committee?"

"They met with Burke over dinner Friday, sir," he reported. "He's on board, and I'm to be his contact person in the Bureau. I'll meet with him this Wednesday."

"Excellent. Have you found someone to work with him?"

"No, sir," Sullivan responded. "But I believe Congressman Conyers has someone in mind. It appears that at the last primary election in Michigan, a former colleague, Harold Ryan, was defeated by another incumbent, Lucian Nedzi, who is a current member of the Judiciary."

Always impatient, Hoover interrupted. "I expect they're just finding a job for one of their own. What do we know of Ryan?"

"He served a couple of terms. He was a team player. And I believe he was a friend of the Bureau when he was in the House. He shouldn't be a problem, sir."

"Good. Keep me informed, Bill."

SILVER SPRING, MARYLAND

After lunch, Ann and Jackie were getting into their pajamas.

"But I'm not tired, Dad," Ann complained.

"We're all just going to rest for a while, girls; me too," Mike coaxed.

"Where is Susan?" Ann probed. "Doesn't she have to rest?"

"Don't worry, young lady. Your sister is going to take a rest, too. She'll be in the living room with Mom."

His two youngest daughters slid under the covers in the downstairs bedroom. He stretched out on the bed alongside them and began to read one of their favorite books, "Green Eggs and Ham."

By the time he finished, both girls had fallen asleep.

He rose carefully from the bed and walked into the living room. There he saw that Susan had fallen asleep, too.

She was on the couch with her mother. Just like her sisters, she had fallen asleep listening to a story, too.

"I guess all that fresh air this morning wore the kids right out," Mike observed.

"I guess. The wet spring has kept us all indoors this year. It was good for them to get out in the sun and run around some. Michael, before we get distracted, let's go into the TV room," Marilyn suggested. "I'd like to finish our discussion about this new assignment of yours."

"Good idea."

They were hardly settled when Marilyn said.

"Are you going to take this assignment?"

"I hardly have a choice, sweetheart."

"You could resign."

"And do what?"

"Work as an accountant. I would think that Baltimore has several firms that could use a well-educated accountant with experience and D.C. connections."

"I haven't used my accounting education since I left college ten years ago. My experience is not in municipal auditing or corporate tax work, either. Besides, I'd be starting at the bottom of the pecking order in any good-sized firm. Working on the Hill, I've built up good contacts, have seniority, and have a wide-open career path. I'm not too keen on leaving government work and starting at the bottom in the private market."

"Would we take a hit on income if you did?" Marilyn asked.

"I don't know, honestly. I haven't checked the market since I worked at the Bureau. Remember, I left that position because you were not comfortable with the culture there. Now, when I'm selected for a plumb investigative assignment, you want me to quit again."

Marilyn bristled at this. "I'm just trying to understand this new assignment, Michael. We're supposed to be working as a team in this marriage. You make it sound like I'm standing in your way and want to control your life."

"Seems like you are, Marilyn. Correct me if I misunderstood, but aren't you the one suggesting I quit my job once again?"

Mike was angry now. He forgot himself and virtually shouted at his wife.

"Crap! I thought you would be happy for the recognition this assignment signifies and the boost to my career on the Hill it promises. Instead, you want me to run from the challenge and quit! I did that the last time you were uncomfortable with my job. But not this time, sweetheart! No sir. Not this time!"

"Lower your voice, Michael. You'll wake the children." Marilyn whispered.

On his way out of the room, Michael snapped. "The children are fine. It's us you really ought to worry about."

I had better get out of here before one of us says something we really regret.

He picked up his briefcase on his way to the living room. Once he settled in a comfortable chair, he opened a copy of the *Warren Commission Report on the Assassination of John F. Kennedy.* He needed to review the 912-page document before he went to the office on Monday.

I might as well get on with it. There's nothing else to do around here until the children wake up.

***

An hour later, he saw his daughter Susan sit up on the couch.

"Is it time to get up yet, Dad?" she asked.

"Sure is, pumpkin," he told her. "I'll bet your sisters are ready to get up, too. Let's go check."

They looked into the front bedroom. Sure enough, Ann was sitting up, looking at the book he had read to them earlier that afternoon. Her sister, Jackie, was awake but still lying under the covers.

Susan pushed the door open.

"Come on, you guys," she said. "Let's go outside. Ya' want to?"

"You bet. Is Dad going, too?" Ann asked.

Just then, her dad stuck his head into the room. "I sure am.

"Up and at 'em, girls, get your shoes on and visit the bathroom. We've got plenty of daylight left for play."

Jackie asked, "Help me with my shoes, Dad? Please."

"Sure, kiddo," he said. "But first, I've got to find the darn things."

Jackie giggled. "They're under the bed, silly."

"Oh, ya'. Why didn't I see them?"

"Susan, ask Mom if she wants to walk over to the park with us, will you?" There was a small park two blocks to the west of their home. The playground equipment provided was swings and teeter-totters. The Burke children loved the swings best.

By the time Mike had gotten her sisters ready for their walk, Susan had rejoined them.

"Mom said she was going to stay home to get dinner ready and for us to be back in one hour."

"OK. We'd better get going then, girls."

The four of them left their house by the front door. From their porch, they saw Joe Zalewski, their next-door neighbor, sitting in his chair on his front porch.

He always sat with his straight-backed chair turned around, resting his arms on the back of the chair as he watched the street. As usual, he was smoking a cigarette.

"Hi, Mr. Joe," Susan shouted. "How are you today?"

"I'm fine, Sue," he responded. "Hi, there, girls. Hi Mike. How are you all today?"

"We're fine, Joe," Mike responded. "How's the street action today? OK?"

Joe was a retired auto worker who spent a good deal of his day watching the street. He had been in this same house since it was built back in 1929.

"It's fine, Mike. The good weather always brings everyone out. I've watched three generations of young families move through this neighborhood. Yours, the Burns and the Young families are the third group to move in at this end of our street. It keeps the street alive, if ya' ask me.

"Being on this porch gives me more enjoyment than anything I could watch on the TV."

"We all appreciate it, too, Joe," Mike assured him. "You ought to charge us a babysitting fee."

"Nope. Can't charge for all the pleasure I get out of watching the kids play."

"We're off to the park, Joe. See you in a bit."

"Have a good time, girls," he said.

"Bye, Mr. Joe," Susan said with a wave.

Jackie was still rather shy, so she didn't join in the banter. Ann was still mad at Joe for shouting at her a week or so ago when she had run toward the street after a ball.

Mr. Joe had been sitting in his usual spot on his front porch when Ann ran by. His shout of warning could have awakened the dead. It stopped her cold. And it sure got Marilyn's attention. Alerted, she came running from the backyard.

Ann received a smack on the bottom from her mother and a time-out on the front porch as her reward. So instead of a greeting, she had a dark look today for Mr. Joe.

He noticed the look and chuckled. He knew she was still angry with him.

***

Mike and the girls left the park in plenty of time to be home as instructed. The only problem was that the playground had puddles and a lot of mud where the swings were. The Burkes used the swings anyway. So, they were covered with mud, even Mike.

On the way back to the house, Susan warned. "Our hands and faces are dirty, and we've all got mud on our shoes and our blue jeans. Mom is gonna be mad."

"But did we have a good time, girls?"

"Yes, yes, yes, we did!" they shouted.

Outside the backdoor, Mike had everyone take off her muddy shoes.

"You guys wait in the TV room for me to get some clean clothes for you."

He went in first.

"We're home, Mom!" he shouted.

Marilyn was in the kitchen setting the table for dinner. She came to the doorway and immediately saw her three muddy daughters standing beside their six-foot-tall and equally muddy father.

She suppressed a laugh. Instead, she put her hands on her hips and frowned.

"Fine thing, Mike. I send them out clean, and you bring them back covered with half the dirt of the park. I can tell you don't have to do laundry around here.

"All right, girls," she continued. "Don't you dare bring any of that dirty stuff into my house. Strip off your clothing, all of it. Mike, run the water in the downstairs tub. You can give the girls a bath while I finish dinner."

"Girls," she concluded. "You might as well get into your pajamas after you wash up. Throw the muddy clothing down the basement, Mike. I'll take care of it later. It's your job to clean their shoes, though. Got it, everyone?"

"We got it, Mom," Mike said. "Right, girls?"

"Right, Dad," the girls responded, almost in unison.

Later that evening, the girls joined their father in the TV room. It was Saturday night, after all, and their special night to stay up late and watch *All In The Family* and the *Mary Tyler Moore* show.

Already in their pajamas, the girls and Mike waited for the other special treat; popcorn.

There were only a few minutes to go until show time. When their mother brought them each a bowl of freshly prepared popcorn, they all dug right in.

"Why don't you join us, Mom?" Mike urged. "I've got a seat for you right here. And there's plenty of popcorn."

"Ya', come on, Mom," the girls joined in.

"No, thanks," she said, as always. "I've got some things I want to do. You go ahead without me."

I can't imagine why she never joins us. It could be such a special time. Oh, well. I can't force her.

WASHINGTON D.C.

It was a bit after 8 a.m. and Burke was at his desk sipping his second coffee. Usually, he spent the first couple of hours of his day preparing for one of the Judiciary Committee's hearings or discussions.

Today would be different for him, though. Today he would begin his new assignment. Finding office space and identifying clerical help were his top priorities.

Possibly, the person hired to assist him would be available, too. He hoped to see him today, if not by the end of the week.

His phone rang. "Mr. Burke," the female on the line said, "I have a Mr. Ryan on line two for you, sir. "

"Thank you," he said and punched the second illuminated button on his desk phone.

"Mike Burke. How can I help you?"

"Mike, this is Harold Ryan. I've been hired to work with you on the review of the Warren Commission's Report."

"Good morning, Harold. Thanks for calling. Are you in D.C.?"

"No, I'm still at Detroit City Airport. My Capital Airlines flight won't get me into D.C. until later today. But I wanted to at least give you a heads up."

"Thanks," Mike responded. "Do you need me to find you a place to stay tonight?"

"No. Congressman Conyers' people got me a room at the Army-Navy Club. How about I meet you in your office tomorrow morning? What is a good time for you?"

"I'm at my desk at eight, Harold. Can you meet me here then?"

"Fine. Anything I should do in the meantime?"

"Do you have a copy of the Report?"

"Yes. Conyers sent me a copy."

"If you could review some of it before our meeting tomorrow, Harold, we can save some time. We meet with our FBI contact on Wednesday. The better prepared we are for that meeting, the better off we'll be."

"I understand," Ryan agreed. "I'll have gone over it by tomorrow morning. See you then."

Just then, a person delivering interoffice memos dropped several onto Burke's desk. One was from Congressman Conyers. Mike opened that one first.

Mike: attached, you will find a bio of Mr. Harold Ryan, who has been retained to work with you.

In addition, contact my secretary at ext. #2103. She will assist you in obtaining office space, telephone, and clerical assistance for your project.

You will also provide her with a proposed plan of work and a budget for my review.

Mike called her immediately. She had already identified office space; two offices and a conference room. She had also found furniture and had ordered phones installed.

She also told him that the clerical pool used by the committee would have to take care of his needs for the time being. She added that she had arranged for his phone lines to be answered by a girl already assigned that duty by the chairman.

OK, Harold, we're ready to hit the road.

SILVER SPRING, MARYLAND

Before he left the office, two copies of the FBI *Report on the Assassination of John F. Kennedy* were delivered from the Government Printing Office. Reading some of that material would be his homework for this evening; after the kids were put to bed.

In the past, when his day went well, he could come home around six p.m. Today, however, he left the office early and arrived home in plenty of time to eat supper with his kids.

"Hi, everyone!" he bellowed, coming into the kitchen by the back door. "Hi, sweetheart." He greeted his wife and gave her a hug.

"Daddy!" His daughters shouted. They ran into the room and hugged his legs.

"This is a nice surprise," Marilyn said after she gave him a perfunctory kiss. "Are you going to make a habit of this?"

"I'd like to, But I don't actually know, Marilyn. With all the interviews we're going to conduct, I expect there will be more late nights than early ones. We may have to travel some, too."

"Will I know any of that in advance?" she asked.

"I expect so. But I'll only be able to put together a schedule as we make appointments. Even so, I should be able to give you one in advance, one week at a time. Last-minute changes will just have to be left to a phone call."

"How do I contact you during the day?"

"I'm told that a switchboard operator in Congressman Conyers' office will handle all my calls. But I'm having a direct line installed tomorrow. I'll get you all the numbers, then."

"That sounds fine, Michael. We can talk after the children are in bed. In the meantime, would you like to join the kids for supper and eat some of their simple fare?"

"What is it, pray tell?" Mike asked.

"Children, tell Dad what we're having for supper."

In virtual unison, the girls shouted, "Marconi and cheese!"

"Yummy: one of my favorites," Mike responded with equal gusto. "Got any applesauce to go with? Be right there, girls," he told them. "Let me wash my hands first."

Later, when the kids were tucked in bed, Mike and Marilyn sat in the living room, each with a cup of coffee. Marilyn opened the conversation.

"So you're off and running with the new assignment."

"It appears so," Mike responded. "All the office arrangements were made today. And I'm to meet my new partner tomorrow morning."

"Is he a Washington guy?"

"He used to be, Marilyn. His name is Harold Ryan. He served two terms as a Congressman from the Detroit area. He was defeated by another incumbent a couple of years ago. Before that, he served a few years as a State Senator in the Michigan Legislature."

"One thing hasn't changed, I see."

"What's that?" Mike asked, on alert for another attack from his wife.

"You brought some work home."

"It's just some reading material, Marilyn. There's nothing new about that. Working for the Judiciary, I frequently brought stuff home to review; you remember."

"Yes, that's true. And you might remember that I didn't like it when you did." Marilyn snapped.

"It was all part of the job, Marilyn.

"I didn't have to bring it with me tonight, though. I had a choice. I could have stayed in the office to go over this material or left the office early enough so that I could join the kids for supper. Would you rather I skipped supper at home and read this material at the office?"

"Not at all, Michael," she responded. "But I had hoped that this assignment would be different."

Will she ever stop?

Mike paused for a moment. "Tell you what, Marilyn," He finally said with a sigh of resignation.

"After I'm done with this investigation, I'll quit. You go teach school full time, and I'll stay home with the kids."

"That's an attractive thought, Michael," Marilyn responded with a laugh. "I'd give you a month, at best, until you went berserk with boredom."

"Are there any other pleasant thoughts you want to share with me tonight, dear?" Mike asked.

NEW YORK TIMES – SEPTEMBER 27, 1964

"The assassination of President Kennedy was the work of one man, Lee Harvey Oswald. There was no conspiracy, foreign or domestic." Warren Commission Report – September 1964

WASHINGTON D.C.

Harold Ryan arrived right on time. He walked into Burke's office at eight a.m., just as he had promised. After the usual greetings were exchanged and coffee cups filled, Mike spoke.

"I see by your bio that we have quite a bit in common, Harold."

"What's that?"

"For starters, we're both Irish Catholic, and it appears that we are both six-feet-two inches tall." Mike stood and looked Ryan in the eye.

"Is there anything besides those two accidents of birth? After all, I'm 57 years old, you know," Ryan asked with a smile.

"Yes, there's that. But we both chose to be educated by the Jesuits. You got your law degree from the University of Detroit, and I earned my bachelor's degree from Boston College."

"Think that will help?" Harold asked.

"We'll soon see," Mike replied.

"I have some reading material for your review, Harold. The five-volume FBI report is on your desk and the summary of the Warren Commission report. I also have a copy of the book by Mark Lane, *Rush to Judgment*, for you."

"Sounds like you have work for me, Mike."

"Last night, I read the testimony Mr. Hoover presented to the Warren Commission on May 14, 1964. You might start with that, too. I've compared the conclusions reached by the FBI and those reached by the Warren Commission. Both investigations insist that Oswald was the only shooter, and both reports denied the existence of a conspiracy. But it's fascinating to me that these two outfits looking at the same information, testimony, and evidence could come up with such a very different conclusion over the number of shots fired, how JFK was killed, and how the governor came to be wounded. I'm anxious to hear your take on this significant difference in the two reports."

"I might as well tell you right now, Mike. I didn't come in here today totally ignorant of the two investigations you referred to or without an opinion. After it hit the best-seller list a few months ago, I took a look at Lane's book. I'm not surprised that it caused such a stir around this town. He tore big holes in both the FBI Report and the Warren Commission Report."

Mike agreed. "True or not, his accusations had something to do with our investigation being authorized."

"I'm not surprised to hear that," Harold continued. "I've handled some criminal cases in my day as an attorney. And I've got to give Lane credit for presenting a very credible defense for his deceased client, Lee Harvey Oswald. I must admit that I'm not the most sought-after defense lawyer in Detroit. But I believe that I could get an acquittal for Oswald if I had at my disposal all the evidence presented by Lane in his book."

"Have you reached any other conclusions, Harold?"

"Yes, I have, Mike," Ryan pressed forward. "Think about this. You are a House committee staffer, and I'm a washed-up politician, a former congressman defeated in a party primary. Just picture it; the two of us are being asked to investigate the crime of the century. And in the process, we're supposed to question the veracity of the Warren Commission, probably the most prestigious blue ribbon panel ever assembled."

"If that weren't difficult and outrageous enough," Ryan continued, "You and I are expected to challenge the word of the most famous and respected crime fighter in American history, J. Edgar Hoover."

"You want to resign before we start, Harold?"

"Shit, no, Mike!" Ryan spit back. "Right now, there's nothing much that separates me from a thousand other Detroit attorneys. Working on this investigation will change that. You see, I'm going to run for the position of Circuit Court Judge this fall. With an Irish name like Ryan and the publicity I'll get out of this investigation, I should be a shoo-in. But what I'm getting at, Mike, is this. Our charge is so broad and the information so voluminous you and I could wallow around with this investigation for years and still come up with nothing new or different. Besides, just like back in 1964, our bosses want us to wrap up our investigation as soon as possible. In fact, no one has any use for us mucking around with this issue into the fall. Do you disagree with me yet?" Ryan asked.

"Not in the least. So what do you suggest?"

"I suggest we disregard the two reports we're being asked to scrutinize. Screw 'em. They were self-serving documents designed to close the door on the subject, not shed light on it, anyway. They started with the assumption that Oswald killed the president and wounded the Texas governor all by himself with a bolt-action relic of a rifle. They also assumed that Oswald, a man who was not a very good shot as a Marine, fired three times within five seconds from a building six floors above the parade route at people sitting in a moving vehicle; and hit human targets with at least two if not all three shots. Do you disagree with that description?"

"No, Harold, I don't."

"So, let's go back to the beginning, the day of the crime, before it was decided that Oswald was the lone shooter. Let's read what the people at Parkland Memorial Hospital said immediately after JFK was brought in. Let's look at the testimony given by witnesses at the scene immediately after the shots were fired. Let's review what critics have said about the Zapruder film and the autopsy data. Let's examine the data from the three re-enactments, too. I'll bet we can show that both the FBI and the Warren Commission ignored or twisted enough information to support their single shooter decision, thus rendering their final reports seriously compromised. We might even give somebody justification to open a full public inquiry."

"Phew!" Mike exclaimed. "Do you always come on this strongly, Harold?"

"Michael, I was in Washington back in '63. I was still a rookie Congressman, but I listened and heard a lot. And what I heard made me believe back then that we didn't get the truth or anything even close about the assassination. Besides, like you, I'm Irish and Catholic. I'm still pissed that they, whoever 'they' are, killed this country's first Irish Catholic president. And I'm angry that these Washington bastards think so little of my intelligence that they expect I should believe the pile of shit contained in these two reports."

"Given how you feel about all of this, why in the hell did Conyers and Ford pick you for this job?"

"They knew me when I was a freshman Congressman back in 1962. I was a go-along, quiet fellow back then. To them, I was just a vote they could depend upon. They would never have picked me for this if they had known me when I was a Michigan State Senator. There was not a go-along thread in my being back then. In fact, following the national census of 1960, the state legislature in Michigan had the task of re-drawing all the election districts. Of course, the Republican majority wanted it to favor their candidates. Representing the Democrats, it was my job to fight them and get the best deal possible for candidates of my political party. When it was finished, those bastards knew they had been in a fight. But during the battle, there was plenty of blood on the floor."

Ryan seemed to have finished.

"I like the way you think and argue a point, Harold. After you left the Michigan legislature and became a congressman, how did you ever lose your bid for re-election in a safe Democratic district?"

"Remember that realignment of election districts I just told you about? Well, the Congressional elections held in 1964 reflected the agreement I had fought about with the Republicans. It just so happened that the district I represented as a congressman had been slated to merge with another congressional district in the Detroit area. So, in the primary of 1964, I had to oppose another Democrat incumbent, a fellow named Lucian Nedzie. He had a pretty good base of Polish votes in a Detroit suburb called Hamtramck. During the wee hours of the morning, after all the votes were cast and supposedly counted, he conceded the election to me. Of course, that doesn't trump votes turning up later from one of his Polish precincts. By eight in the morning, I discovered I had lost the election by less than 100 votes."

"Sounds like something out of Lyndon Johnson's Texas election playbook or Mayor Dailey's Chicago deal. Didn't you challenge the tally?"

"They used paper ballots in Hamtramck at that time. It's during the initial counting that you need to watch for an honest count in a situation like that."

"So why didn't you?"

"We couldn't find people who were willing to be poll watchers at those precincts, not even for pay. Everyone was afraid to go there. The women who ran those precincts on Election Day had one tough reputation."

"Sounds like the fix was in."

"Maybe so. I tried again in the primary of 1966. But that time around, Lucian was the incumbent. As such, he had the support of the Unions and beat me handily."

"Any bitterness, Harold?"

"I talked with Sam Fishman about it. He was in charge of such things for the United Auto Workers. He told me that I'll have their support when I run for Wayne County Circuit Judge this fall. So I put all that old stuff behind me," Harold declared. "Being a circuit judge is a lot easier than a congressman, believe me. Besides, Lucian is an honest, intelligent man. He'll do a good job for the district."

"Good to hear it." Mike changed the subject.

"About this investigation of ours, I tend to agree with your line of thinking, Harold. "So I suggest we spend this afternoon mapping out two agendas for our investigation – one for Conyers, Ford, the FBI, and public consumption, and another one just for us; a hidden agenda, as they say on the Hill."

Ryan laughed heartily. "I get your meaning, Burke. I believe we're going to get along nicely."

Mike chuckled. "I think so too, Harold, but your tirade has gotten me so excited I've got to visit the men's room before we start."

OFFICES OF THE FEDERAL BUREAU OF INVESTIGATION

"Mr. Sullivan will see you now, gentlemen." an aide to the Assistant Director told them.

"Please follow me." Burke and Ryan stood and were led down to the end of a long, dimly lit hallway. They were then shown into a rather unpretentious office, and the door shut behind them.

"Good morning, Mike," Sullivan greeted, shaking Burke's outstretched hand. "Good to see you again." He then turned to Harold Ryan and shook his hand, too. "Nice to meet you, Congressman Ryan."

It was common practice to address former members of Congress by their elected title.

"Have a seat at the conference table, please," he directed.

Once the three men were seated, Sullivan asked, "How can I help your investigation?"

"May we take notes, Director?" Mike asked his old boss.

"Of course, Mike."

Ryan asked the first question. "Sir, in his May 1964 statement to the Commission, Mr. Hoover stated that President Kennedy was killed and Governor Connally wounded by three shots from Oswald's rifle; that there were no other shooters."

"That's correct, Congressman." Sullivan agreed.

"How did your people arrive at that conclusion?" Ryan continued.

"Our trained experts simply followed the evidence, gentlemen."

If Ryan had expected a fuller answer, he would be disappointed. There was an embarrassing silence instead.

"What evidence was that, sir?" Ryan pressed.

"First, the Dallas police quickly identified Oswald as the shooter. Secondly, ballistics tied his rifle to both victims. And third, the autopsy revealed that all the shots which struck the victims came from behind the motorcade and the sixth floor of the Depository Building, where shell casings and Oswald's fingerprints were found. It left our people with no choice but to conclude the findings you can read in our report of December 1963."

Mike asked, "Director, has any evidence surfaced since the FBI Report of December 1963 was issued to change that finding?"

"Despite the fact that our agents have continued to pursue new leads and collect additional information, we have found nothing to change the findings expressed in the Bureau's December 1963 Report."

"I see, sir. Would it be possible to interview the personnel who conducted the investigation immediately following the shooting?" Mike asked.

"As you might understand, Mike," Sullivan responded. "The agents assigned that task have been assigned elsewhere and to other investigations. Some are probably no longer even with the Bureau. But I expect a few of them are still in the D.C. area. I will check it out and make them available to you and Congressman Ryan."

"That would be helpful, sir," Burke said. "We can be contacted at this number." Mike handed Sullivan a business card.

"Do either of you have any more questions for me this morning?"

Mike and Harold looked at one another and shook their heads.

"No, sir," Burke said. "We appreciate the time you have given us."

"As your investigation continues, gentlemen," Sullivan told them, "do not hesitate to call me if you think I can be of any more help. Mr. Hoover has promised the leadership of the Judiciary Committee our complete cooperation."

The three men stood and shook hands. "Thank you, sir," Mike said.

"It was good to see you, Mike," Sullivan said. "And it was a pleasure to meet you, Congressman."

***

Over a sandwich at their desk, the two investigators shared impressions of their first encounter with the Federal Bureau of Investigation.

"What do you think, Harold?"

"We would have been better off sleeping in this morning. Our questions were not sufficiently challenging, nor were Sullivan's answers enlightening."

"I disagree," Mike replied. "We asked the two questions you and I decided we had to ask. If they weren't the right ones or properly put, shame on us. But they had to be asked. And, they were better asked at the outset, too."

"I suppose," Ryan reluctantly agreed.

"As for Sullivan's responses," Mike continued. "He didn't rise to Assistant Director of the FBI, the number three guy in the Bureau, by forgetting the official line contained in their December 1963 Report, or by stumbling over delivering it."

"He was smooth, all right," Ryan admitted. "He even looked as though he believed it."

"He does, Harold. Like most career agents, as I once was, Assistant Director Sullivan is a true believer. He does not harbor a shred of doubt that anything his Bureau says officially might not be correct. In his testimony before the Warren Commission, Mr. Hoover set the scene. He stated as a fact that Oswald was the only shooter and that there was no conspiracy. He told the members of the commission that any criticism of either the FBI Report or the Warren Commission would come from 'extremists' and have no foundation in fact. Remember, Harold," Mike continued. "The culture at the Bureau is that Mr. Hoover is always correct."

"Well then, I suppose they'd like us to just pack our bags, lock the doors and go home," Harold said.

"I suppose. But it's not going to happen, my friend. We've got too much work to do. Look at the list we put together yesterday," Burke urged.

"It is enormous," Ryan judged. "It would take us a year and a staff of dozens to sift through all of this."

Burke broke in, "So, instead of tackling the entirety of the data collected from all sources, why don't we focus on two issues?"

"Which are?" Harold asked.

"The directionality of the shots and the number of shots that could possibly have been fired from the Italian-made rifle the commission used in their reenactments."

Ryan jumped on that. "Sure. That makes sense. If we find no foundation for the single bullet theory, determine that the throat wound was one of entry and that the shot to the president's head came from the front, the whole house of cards crumbles. Because if the assassination had to be accomplished by more than one shooter, the basis of both reports would be compromised, and their cover-up exposed. I love it."

Burke added, "And it's something you and I can accomplish in a reasonable amount of time."

"Exactly."

"So, I'm going to look into all the ballistic information, the Zapruder film, and the crime scene reconstruction data," Burke determined.

"And I've got a stack of testimony on the Dallas emergency room response and the Bethesda Hospital autopsy to review," Ryan summarized.

"Right. We will also need to conduct interviews with a good sampling of Dealey Plaza witnesses."

"Well, then, Mike," Harold urged. "I suggest we get to it. Let's each spend the rest of the day examining the available data, list our interview targets, get a good night's sleep, and exchange notes at an eight o'clock meeting tomorrow morning."

"Sounds like a plan to me," Mike said. "Later this afternoon, I'll try to catch the four o'clock 16th Street bus up Atlanta Avenue to the District Line Terminal. If I can make all the connections, I'll be home in time to eat with the kids."

"Do it, Mike," Harold urged him. "Reminds me of when my kids were young. Unfortunately, there were more nights that I didn't make it home in time than I care to remember. That was my loss, for sure. Oh, well, that's water over the dam. Good luck with making all the connections. I'll lock up when I'm done; see you in the morning."

With that, Ryan went into his office and shut the door.

FEDERAL BUREAU OF INVESTIGATION

Toward the conclusion of his meeting with his assistant directors, Mr. Hoover asked James Sullivan a question.

"How did your meeting today with Burke and Ryan go, Jim?"

"It went pretty much as I expected, sir," Jim answered. He then reviewed the line of questioning taken and his answers.

"Impressions?"

"They won't be any trouble. The task they face is enormous. They're being pressed to finish quickly and to do so with very limited resources. I don't expect them to come up with much."

"Keep me apprised, Jim."

"Yes, sir."

SILVER SPRING, MARYLAND

Mike walked into the TV room by the back door a few minutes before five o'clock. His daughter Jackie was playing with her Barbie doll house on the floor of the room.

"Daddy!" she shouted in surprise.

"Hi, little girl," he said as he stooped to pick her up.

"Hi, everyone!" he shouted as the two walked into the kitchen.

"Three nights in a row," his wife greeted him. "That must be some kind of record, amazing." She gave him a peck as he walked by with their youngest daughter in his arms.

"Understandable, I'm amazing, don't ya' know."

That boast was greeted with a cheerful, "Aren't you full of it tonight."

Susan and Ann were playing dolls on the floor of the living room.

"Daddy!" they shouted and grabbed his legs.

"Have you eaten yet, girls?"

Marilyn had followed him into the room; she answered.

"No, they haven't," she told him. "They're about to, though. Why don't you sit with them while they eat? You and I can have our dinner after they have their bath."

"Sounds good to me," Mike agreed.

At the table, Ann wasn't eating her peas.

"Hey, young lady," her dad asked, "What about those peas?"

"I don't like peas."

"Remember the rule?" Mike asked her. "

Susan jumped into the conversation. "Oh ya,' Dad. Do you mean the 'no thank you taste' rule?"

"That's the one. Ya' need to take a taste before you can refuse something on your plate."

"What if I didn't want the stuff in the first place?"

"Because Mom thought it would be good for you. Now, it's up to you to have a taste. If you don't like it, she won't put any on your plate next time. Does that seem fair, Annie?"

"I suppose," Ann responded reluctantly.

"Well?" her father waited. "A taste?"

Ann put a spoonful of peas into her mouth, chewed, and swallowed. "Ugg!" she declared. "They're awful."

"Now you know," Mike announced.

After their bath, the children were in bed, waiting for their father to tell them a story.

"Tell us when you were a little boy, Dad," Jackie pleaded.

"Well, let me see," he began, pretending to be deep in thought.

"Tell us about sleeping in the attic," Ann begged.

"Haven't I told you that one before?" he asked.

"I like that one, too," Susan said.

"All right," he agreed. "Well, when I was a little boy, my brother Joe, who everyone called Buddy, and I slept together in this huge room up in the attic of my grandparent's home. All the bedrooms on the second floor had people in them; two aunts in one, my mother and father in another, and my grandparents in a third. Our little brother David slept in a fourth small bedroom. My uncle John slept with us up in the attic, too, except he was away in the Navy during a big war that was going on."

Jackie sat up and asked, "What's an attic? I forgot."

"Your bedroom is on the second floor, right? Some really big houses have a floor on top of the second floor. There's a stairway to it just like the one we use to get up here. That third floor is called an attic. OK?"

"Now I remember," Jackie said, laying back on her pillow with her thumb in her mouth and her blankie held against her face.

"Anyway," he continued, "one night after our mother turned off the light, it was very, very dark. Suddenly, a white flash appeared in the window right by our bed. It was quickly followed by a loud bang!"

He made a loud bang by clapping his hands together. Surprised by the noise he had made, his girls jumped and huddled closer together under the blankets.

"A thunderstorm had begun. Then it began to rain. The wind drove the rain against the window and onto the roof. The thunder and lightning continued, and it was all so loud we could hardly hear each other talk. We couldn't sleep either. So we huddled under the covers and hoped the glass in the window didn't break and let in all the rain."

"What happened next, Dad?" Jackie asked.

"I guess we fell asleep. Because when I woke up, the rain had stopped, and the sun was shining."

"Tell us another story, Dad," Ann asked.

"That's enough for tonight, girls. It's time for sleep."

***

Mike quietly went down the steep staircase to the living room.

Marilyn was sitting on the couch, reading. He sat next to her, so she put down the book and looked at him.

"The girls love those 'when I was a little boy' stories you tell them, Michael," Marilyn told him.

"I hope I don't run out of them."

"I expect you'll think of something." Marilyn chuckled.

"You have some important evening reading, do ya'?" Mike asked with a smirk on his face.

"Are you trying to be funny? That's my line," Marilyn responded with a smirk of her own.

Mike slid closer and put his arm around his wife.

"I decided to leave my work at the office and come home early. What do you think of that, little lady?"

"I think it was a wise decision, mister," Marilyn said, snuggling closer.

"I told you I was amazing."

"Did you have anything special in mind tonight instead of reading?" She ran her hand up his thigh.

In his best Humphrey Bogart impersonation, Mike said, "That depends on what you have for supper, sweetheart?"

"Prepared especially for you, I have warmed-up meatloaf, fried potatoes from the other night, and gravy out of a bottle. I also have a slice of chocolate cake saved from the kid's supper."

"I can't wait. I love left-over meatloaf. But first, how about an appetizer?"

"What might that be?"

"We can make love before we eat."

"Do I have a choice?"

"Yes, you do," Mike continued as he began to unbutton his wife's blouse. She didn't resist.

"We can make love on this couch or retire to the comfortable bed in the down-stairs guest room."

"Wow! I'm overwhelmed. Do I have any other choices?"

Marilyn's blouse fell to the floor.

"Yes. You may shower first or make love as you are."

Mike's hands began to explore as he kissed his wife's neck

What his hands were doing brought a flush to her cheeks. "What if I already showered before you arrived home?" she whispered.

Mike looked surprised. "Are you telling me that my amazing seductive moves weren't necessary?"

She answered with a long wet kiss.

"You're the big shot investigator, Michael. You figure it out."

Phew! What a woman! I don't think we're going to warm up that meatloaf after all.

Marilyn slid out of his arms and slowly stood. By the time she turned completely around, her bra had fallen to the floor.

"Aren't you glad you came home early, big fella?"

They never made it to that comfortable bed, either.

WASHINGTON, D.C,

Ryan was already in the office when Mike arrived at his usual time.

"Did you even go to your room last night, Harold?"

"Yes, I did. I had a drink and a delicious T-bone steak in the Officer's Club's dining room and was in bed early, too. But I was awake early this morning, so I walked over here around six. I'm on my second cup of coffee. Help yourself, Mike. I made plenty."

"Good thing," Mike responded. "I got a late start, so I need a cup. What's the schedule for this morning?"

"I suggest we work separately this morning, go out for lunch and then compare notes this afternoon."

"Good," Mike responded. "Last evening was a family night. So I didn't get a thing done at home. I need some time to review a few things before we meet."

So that's what they did. After lunch, however, they were both eager to share the conclusions of their study.

***

Burke and Ryan met in the conference room they shared with several other staffers housed on their floor.

"You go first, Harold."

"All right," he agreed. "I think we need to go right at all the physical evidence about the wounds, starting with what was seen at Parkland Memorial Hospital immediately after the shooting. First, I intend to talk with the Parkland Memorial Hospital trauma doctors Clark, Charles Crenshaw, Perry, and McClelland. There may be some others, but I'll start with these men. They were the ones in the Trauma Room at Parkland who tried to save the president's life. Their initial trauma room observations told a different story than that presented by the Commission. I'd like to see if they have changed their November 22nd observations. I'll also talk with Dr. Rose, the pathologist who was prevented by Secret Service people from doing an autopsy after JFK was declared dead. Back in D.C., I'll talk with Admiral G. Burkley, JFK's White House physician. He was with the president in Dallas and signed the death certificate while still at Parkland Memorial Hospital on November 22nd. He was also present at the Bethesda Hospital autopsy. Once I've done that, I'll interview the Bethesda Hospital doctors who examined the president's body and conducted the official autopsy. I think it critical for us to first plow through all the commission testimony and documents dealing with the physical evidence. I believe we must do this before we can draw any conclusions about the angle and direction of the shots fired in Dallas on November 22nd."

"Do you agree, Mike?"

"Absolutely. Do you need any help with that?"

"Not right now. If I get swamped with the information from all the medical people, I'll gladly take some help. But right now, I think you should spend your time on the forensic stuff. There's so much of that, you'll probably need my help."

"We'll see," Mike said. "If you're done for now, are you ready for my report?"

"Yes. Go ahead."

Mike began. "I think I must go to the heart of the public uproar concerning the two reports. It's pretty obvious that the Warren Commission agreed with the FBI that Oswald was the lone shooter and that there was no conspiracy, foreign or domestic. But they did not agree about the number of hits scored by the shooter. So I think I'll start with that. That means I must interview Arlan Specter first. He was the commission lawyer who came up with the single bullet theory. I'm going to see him in Philadelphia next week. Bill Sullivan at the Bureau promised to cooperate and get me the names of the FBI team who decided all three shots hit human targets; two hitting the president and one wounding the governor. I'll interview them. Governor and Mrs. Connally will be next. His testimony before the commission clearly refutes the 'single bullet' approach the commissioners took.

After I take their testimony, I'll spend some time in Dallas talking with Michael West. With help from a fellow named Breneman, West set up all three of the assassination re-enactments; the one staged by *Time-Life* in November, the one staged by the FBI in December, and the last one staged for the Warren Commission in May of 1964. When I called Mr. West for an appointment, he said it was about time someone in Washington wanted to talk with him and Breneman about the reenactments."

Harold interrupted, "Dollars to donuts, I bet you find that the data those two guys developed was different from the data used by the Warren Commission to support their insistence that a single bullet hit both Kennedy and Connally. I'm anxious to hear what these guys have to say."

"I am too, Harold."

"I have a suggestion, Mike," Ryan said. "I suggest you see West and Breneman first. Then, if you discover that the data was falsified, you'll know it before you talk with Specter.

"Besides, with our thin budget, if we do our Texas interviews together, we can room together in Dallas."

"Good point. I can do Dallas first. Not a problem. I'll call Specter and change the appointment."

Burke continued, "I've already made appointments with the Dallas Police Chief, Jesse Curry, and the County Sheriff, Joe Decker. Both men were riding in the lead car of the motorcade. Curry has publicly said some very interesting things which are at odds with both the FBI Report and the Commission Report. As for Sheriff Decker, immediately after the shooting, he ordered personnel from his office to secure the railroad yard and the area behind the wooden fence because he suspected shots came from there. So I'll talk with them. I'm told they have accumulated quite a bit of eyewitness testimony never presented to the Commission. I also have an appointment to talk with the Book Depository Building superintendent, Roy Truly. He and a police officer named Baker saw Oswald standing in the second-floor lunchroom drinking a Coke a minute or two after the last shot was fired."

"That will be an interesting interview, Mike," Ryan decided.

"You got that right. After I'm finished in Texas, I'll visit with who set up the shooting re-enactment for the Warren Commission, then Specter in Pennsylvania. Then, I'll see three of the Warren Commission members, Senator Russell, Senator Cooper, and Congressman Hale Boggs. All three initially refused to sign off on the 'single bullet' theory. But they eventually signed the report anyway. I'd like to know why they changed their minds."

"Why don't you let me talk with those three, Mike?" Ryan suggested. "I worked some with Boggs when I was in the House. I might get more out of him and the other two."

"Sounds good. You handle that after we return from Texas?"

"Yes."

"I have a copy of the *Life Magazine* issue showing the assassination from the Zapruder film, frame by frame. But I'd like to find some technical people to walk us through Mr. Zapruder's copy of that film. In his book *Rush to Judgment,* Mark Lane contends that the film was altered to support Specter's single bullet theory."

"Why don't you just call Lane?" Ryan asked. "He might be willing to share his sources on the film with us."

Burke was taking notes. "Good idea. I'll do just that."

"And finally," Burke resumed, "before we wrap up gathering information for our report, I believe we need to review all of the eyewitness testimony that was given to the Commission along with that given to the Dallas officials."

"You think some of that testimony was overlooked by the Commission?" Harold asked.

"Maybe it was, and maybe it wasn't, Harold. But I think we need to check it out. Who knows, maybe they ignored any testimony that contradicted or undermined their single bullet, lone shooter theory."

"Maybe they did, and maybe they didn't," Harold concluded. "Let's see where all the evidence takes us."

***

Burke and Ryan spent the rest of the day and the next, arranging their trip to Dallas. The House's Judiciary Committee switchboard personnel were a great help in contacting people and setting the schedule for the Texas trip.

At the end of the second day, Friday, the two investigators had a full schedule of interviews. They would leave for Dallas the following Monday.

SILVER SPRING, MARYLAND

All was quiet in the Burke household. The kids were asleep. Mike and Marilyn were enjoying coffee in the TV room.

"So you'll be staying with Ryan at the Dallas Howard Johnson's motel."

"That's right. Sharing a room will save us some money. The motel is very new and has a restaurant attached, so that will be convenient. It's just off the North Central Expressway. That should make it pretty convenient. We've got a government vehicle assigned to us, as well."

"You expect to be there a full week?" Marilyn asked.

"I'm afraid so. Look at that schedule I gave you. The Judiciary staff scheduled enough interviews for us in the Dallas area alone to nearly take a week to accomplish. I expect to fill in some of the gaps when we get there, too. I don't look forward to being away that long, but best get it over with rather than have to fly down there again."

"I suppose," Marilyn agreed. "You've never been away from us for that long, you know. Can't you conduct your interviews over the phone?"

"Some will have to be made by phone, I'm sure, sweetheart. But whenever possible, we need to look people in the eye when we question them. This is not a pleasure trip. It will be all work and no play, I assure you."

"It better be, Buster. I don't want to see your picture all over the news cavorting in Jack Ruby's Dallas strip club."

"Come to think of it, we might have to interview a couple of his dancers there."

"What?" Marilyn sat up straight, ready for a fight.

"No, sweetheart," Mike protested. "I'm only kidding."

"You had better be, or God help you."

Mike set his empty cup on the floor and joined his wife on the couch. "Will you miss me?"

"The children will."

"What about their mother?" He put his arm around his wife and pulled her close.

"That depends."

"On what?"

"How she feels after you've been gone a few days."

They kissed. Then they went on to other things.

ST. LOUIS POST-DISPATCH - DECEMBER 1963

"At the time of the shooting, the president's automobile was moving almost directly away from the window from which the shots are thought to have been fired...Motion pictures of the president's car, made public after a few days'delay, made it clear that all the shots were fired after the president had made the turn and passed the building. If the shots came from the sixth-floor window, they came from almost directly behind the president."

DALLAS, TEXAS

Michael Burke was using one of the conference rooms at FBI headquarters in Dallas. Mike's contact in the Bureau, Mr. Paul Sullivan, had arranged for its use.

Mike was not concerned that the room was most likely bugged. After all, this was not a judicial proceeding where witnesses were sworn or represented by attorneys. These would be just informal meetings. Besides, he was going to tape each interview, too.

His first interview of the day was with Michael West, who had set up the November 26, 1963, re-enactment of the assassination for Time-Life. West was the Dallas County Surveyor. He was joined by Chester Breneman, a surveyor who worked with him on the re-enactments.

Burke had made copies of the Dallas Morning News rendering of Dealey Plaza and the surrounding roads for their use during this interview.

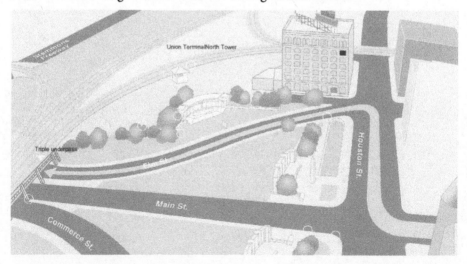

"Good morning, Mr. West, Mr. Breneman," Burke greeted. "Thank you for coming."

"You're most welcome," West said. "Since Chet and I set up the two government assassination re-enactments, I was surprised that neither of us was ever called to explain the implications of the measurements we took for those two surveys."

"You can do that now, gentlemen. For the record, please explain the purpose of such a survey," Burke asked.

"As with many of our investigations following a murder, the purpose of such a survey is to precisely measure the crime scene to determine bullet trajectories and directionality," West said.

Burke asked. "What did you do in your work on the Kennedy assassination?"

"We took measurements of the plaza and noted distances from the Book Depository Building and then matched all these against the stills of the Zapruder film," Breneman answered.

"Do you do this in all murder cases?"

"No. In most murders, the autopsy gives us most of the information. But in this case, the victim's body was not subjected to an official autopsy as Texas law demands. Instead, the Feds took the president's body to Washington at gunpoint."

"Didn't the doctors at Parkland Hospital have the forensic information you needed?"

"The Parkland Hospital people were primarily concerned with trying to save the life of President Kennedy, not performing an autopsy."

"So the forensic evidence, usually available, was absent?"

"Correct. In the case of the Kennedy assassination, we had to look elsewhere. So the measurements taken for our survey, matched with the Zapruder film, were used to help investigators determine directionality and thus whether or not the killing was committed by one or multiple shooters."

"The medical people at Bethesda Hospital testified that all the wounds to the president were caused by shots from behind him," Burke prompted.

"I don't know anything about that autopsy, Mr. Burke," West commented. "All I know is that our surveys did not support that conclusion. In fact, after we studied the results of the November 29th survey with the *Life Magazine* investigators, we all agreed that no one person could have done all the shooting," Breneman said.

"Wouldn't that mean that investigators studying the results of all the re-enactments would have come to the same conclusion?" Burke asked.

"One would think that to be true, Mr. Burke," West surmised. "But that did not happen. Elements contained in the government studies were different than those present in the *Life Magazine* study. For example, the Secret Service used a Lincoln limo with bench seats, not jump seats, as was the case in Kennedy's Lincoln vehicle. With bench seats, it was possible to place Governor Connally far enough to the left to allow a single bullet to strike both the president and the governor. With jump seats, though, the governor would have had to be seated on his right buttock at the far left edge of his seat to the left of the president when struck."

Chester Breneman added, "But the Zapruder film clearly shows him seated to the right, directly in front of the president."

"So, in the Secret Service study, the re-enactors were not seated the same as were the victims on November 22nd," West added.

"Another difference," Breneman interjected, "was that during the *Life Magazine* study, I noticed three still photographs taken from the Zapruder film that showed blood and brain matter virtually flying out of the president's head toward the rear of his limo. But, the stills of those images were missing from the film we were told to use for the government surveys. Another difference," Brenneman continued, "For the May re-enactment, Mr. Specter had brought this big old Cadillac limo down to use in the tests. It was thirteen inches higher than Kennedy's Lincoln limo. And, they (the re-enactors) were all crunched up shoulder to shoulder in the car seats. That situation made it more possible for one man to wound two passengers with one bullet. Also, both of these vehicles sit at different heights off the ground than the vehicle Kennedy rode in on November 22nd. In the re-enactment vehicles, the president would have sat much higher and therefore been much more exposed than he actually was. As a result, all the angles were different than on November 22nd."

"In addition," West said, "Specter had his three marksmen firing at a stationary target from a platform that was only thirty feet above the ground. The window from which the alleged shooter fired was sixty feet above the ground, and the shooter would have been firing at a moving target. All of these differences affect the angles of the bullets fired, you see. Because of these differences, in my view, Mr. Burke," West concluded. "Only the *Life Magazine* re-enactment of November 1963 was anywhere near accurate. The Warren Commission never looked at the results of that study."

"Do you have any idea why they didn't at least do that?"

"I can only guess, Mr. Burke. But if I were pressed to answer that question, I'd say that the *Life* study didn't support the early conclusion the FBI made that all the shots were fired by a single shooter from the sixth-floor window of the Book Depository Building. Later in 1964, I'd say they didn't look at the *Life* study because it didn't support Specter's single bullet theory. So it was simply ignored."

"Are you also saying, Mr. West," Burke persisted, "that none of the three surveys supported the Warren Commission's or the FBI's single shooter theory or the single bullet theory?"

"Now you have it, Mr. Burke," Chester Breneman said. "In addition, when we were going to include the bullet strike on the south curb of Elm in our plat map, the FBI told us to ignore it, not to include it."

"The FBI didn't want what appeared to be a fourth shot included because it countered the three shot, single shooter conclusion of their December 1963 Report?" Burke asked.

"Exactly. That appeared to be more important than the truth."

"Also," West went on, "none of the survey data which we developed for any of the re-enactments was presented to the members of the Commission. In fact, Mr. Specter didn't even open the container in which we sent our results of the May 24, 1964 study we did for the Commission. They didn't see the plat map or the legend that explained it. It was never even examined. He had Chief Justice Warren seal it. The re-enactment information presented by Mr. Specter to the members of the Commission was different than what we developed for their May 24th survey."

"It sure was," Breneman said. "For instance, on our map, we marked the spot corresponding to Zapruder film frame 171. The Warren Commission changed this to 166 before they used it in the report. The Warren Report shows a 210 frame, where we show a 208…It would seem to me that…these figures were changed just enough so that the Warren Commission could support their contention that a second shot came from the same direction as the first; from behind."

"It was altered?"

"I know what we sent Specter," West concluded. "And I assure you it wasn't what he presented to the Commission."

"You believe it was made up to support his single bullet theory, then?" Burke asked.

"That's it exactly, Mr. Burke."

***

Sheriff Decker was next on the schedule. He was late.

"Good morning, Sheriff," Mike greeted. "Thank you for coming. Please have a seat. Can I get you some coffee?"

"No, on the coffee, Burke," Decker snapped. "Will this business take us very long? I've got some constructive work to do this morning."

"I'll try not to take long, Sheriff," Mike responded. Then he turned on the tape recorder.

"What in hell is that for, Burke?"

Mike turned off the machine. Then he leaned across the table, paused, looked the Dallas County sheriff in the eye, and spoke.

"Would you rather I subpoena your arrogant ass? Then you'd have to appear in a publicly televised session of the entire House Judiciary Committee in Washington. I assure you that you will not receive a friendly reception. But, it's your choice, Sheriff Decker."

Mike sat back and silently waited for a reply.

Decker laughed loudly and slapped his open hand on the table in front of him. "All right, Burke. Ya' got me there. Let's get on with this. What do you want to know?"

Well, I'll be. This bastard was just testing me.

Burke turned on the tape recorder and asked, "Please describe what you saw while riding in the lead car of the president's motorcade on November 22nd 1963."

"I sat in the back seat of a four-door sedan. Dallas Chief of Police Curry, Secret Service agents Winston Larson and Forrest Sorrels were also in the vehicle. The president's limo had just made the turn behind us onto Elm when I heard a shot. Instinctively, I looked right, to the sound of the shot. When I did, I saw a bullet glance off the pavement behind us and to the right. Motorcycle Officer Chaney saw that, too; I found out later. I also saw some smoke by the fence on the Grassy Knoll. I got on the car's radio to my office and ordered, and this is almost word for word, Burke. Move all available men out of my office into the railroad yard...and hold everything secure until Homicide and other investigators should get there."

"Did anyone else in your vehicle hear the shot or see the smoke on the Grassy Knoll?"

"I wasn't concerned with what anyone else saw or heard, Burke. You'll have to ask them. Cus' within seconds of my order, my vehicle was leading the way to Parkland Hospital."

Mike changed the focus, "I read testimony Sheriff, that on the morning of November 22nd, you ordered your deputies, and this is word for word too, "...take no part whatsoever in the security of the presidential motorcade. Why would you issue such an order?"

"I issued it because, late the night before, the Secret Service people ordered us to stand down. They decided my people weren't needed; they told Chief Curry the same thing. Out at Love Field the next morning, they ordered our motorcycle policemen not to ride alongside the presidential limo but to follow it instead."

"Who told your mounted officers to follow behind the limo?"

"I was told that it was Winston Larson.

"Another thing, Burke," Decker went on, in full rage now. "As we approached the underpass, Larson was all upset when he saw people standing along the top, right over the approaching motorcade. We could've secured all the windows in the buildings facing Elm Street as well as cleared the overpass of onlookers, just like they did in Fort Worth for the parade that was held there earlier that morning. I just had guys standin' around watching the parade, for God's sake. The Secret Service turned down all sorts 'a help. That includes the help the military police offered, too. The arrogant Secret Service bastards said they had the parade route covered. But, all during the drive from Love Field, I heard Larsen and Sorrels complain about how tired their agents were and about not having enough a' them. Hell, they had enough agents to assign some ta' guard the head table at the site of the lunch in the Trade Mart instead of the parade route. Don't get me started on those sons 'a bitches, Burke. Seems ta' me they set the president up as an easy target. An' they have the nerve to imply that our city was somehow responsible for the tragedy. Pisses me off, let me tell you."

AUSTIN, TEXAS

Burke rang the bell at the front door of the Connally home a few minutes before his eleven o'clock morning appointment.

A formally dressed gentleman opened the door.

"Good morning, sir," the man began. "Are you Mr. Burke?"

"Yes, I am," he responded. "Am I too early for my appointment with Governor and Mrs. Connally?"

"Not at all, sir. Please come in. While you're waiting in the sitting room, I'll let the governor's secretary know you're here."

"Thank you," Burke said as he was led into a room off the hallway.

It wasn't long before Governor Connally's appointment secretary came into the room.

"Good morning, Mr. Burke," she said. "The governor told me to bring you back as soon as you arrived."

"Thank you."

"Please follow me."

On the second floor, he was led into a much larger sitting room. The governor did not rise to greet him. But Mrs. Connally did.

"Welcome to my home, Mr. Burke," she greeted. "Please have a seat."

Once Burke was seated, the governor asked, "Can I assume you've read the statements Nellie and I gave to the Warren Commission almost three years ago?"

"Yes, sir," Burke responded. "I've read both of them."

"Are you here on the chance that one of us has changed our recollection of that terrible few seconds in Dallas?"

"Well, sir," Burke began. "Now that you bring that up, do either of you wish to add or change that testimony?"

"I don't," the governor responded without hesitation. "What about you, Nellie?"

"I don't wish to change a word of what I said back then," Mrs. Connally answered.

"Actually, I could expand some on what I said about hearing the first shot. When testifying, I said that the velocity of a bullet is such that it will have reached its target by the time you hear it. During my recovery, I had plenty of time to talk to people and read about that phenomenon. I found that I was correct," added the governor.

Mrs. Connally jumped into the conversation. "The FBI report was correct. John was hit by the second bullet fired, a separate bullet. This business about a single bullet striking both the president and John is a bunch of hooey."

"Do you know why the Warren Commission members adopted it, sir?"

"I suspect that it was a lawyer's concoction to close down the investigation and speed up the completion of the formal report before the fall's presidential election. Hell's fire, I thought that was an open secret around Washington. So why are you really here, young fella?"

"I'm here to ask you one question, Governor."

"Must be a damned important question for y'all to come all the way from our nation's capital ta ask it. Go ahead, Mr. Burke, ask your question."

"Why did you insist on changing the route of the presidential parade, sir?"

Governor Connally's face reddened. "Why in the damn hell would I care about a stupid parade route? I was the governor of Texas. Do you think that's all I had to concern myself with back then?"

"No, sir," Burke said, taken aback at the ferocious response, "I have no opinion on the matter. But Mr. Bruno, who was Kenny O'Donnell's advance man, said he was in your office when you called the White House and insisted on the route change from Main Street to Elm Street. O'Donnell confirms the call and the issue discussed."

"And he agreed with me," Connally interjected. "That the Elm Street route was a more direct route to the Trade Mart luncheon site."

"Yes sir, he did," Burke confirmed.

Burke pressed on, "But Mr. O'Donnell and his advance man Bruno wanted the safer and more traditional route down Main Street. President Kennedy intervened and told him that you and the vice-president were to control the Dallas visit, including the parade."

Once again, Governor Connally interrupted, "And, if you check it out, Mr. Burke, the Secret Service people signed off on the change, too."

"Yes, sir. They did. But Governor," Burke continued, "why did you insist on a change in the route from Main Street to Elm Street?"

"Persistent Yankee, isn't he, Nellie?" Connally said, smiling. Having lightened the charged atmosphere somewhat, the governor asked, "Have you ever worked in a political campaign, Burke?"

"No, sir. I have not."

"Let me tell ya' then. At all levels of campaigning, there are issues of territory and ownership. If someone barges into your territory, even if it's to help, there's usually resentment. Now then, when someone asks for your help and then tries to dictate as well, it is really resented. The locals then sort a' push back some and flex their muscle, as it were. So, in the fall of 1963, there was a bunch a' rather snotty Eastern liberals fixin' to come into my territory. They needed my help to get the folks of Texas to vote for their candidate for president in 1964. As silly as it sounds in light of the terrible things that happened in Dallas, we had a bit of a pissing contest, me an' those Eastern boys. And it came down to who was in charge of a God-damned parade route and lunch site. I've thought of the what-ifs, a' that whole business, and regretted it more times than I can count. Does that answer your damned question, Burke?"

"Yes, sir, it does. I'm sorry I had to ask it.

"Could I ask one final question, sir?"

"Might as well," Connally was visibly tired but said," Go ahead."

"According to a Harris-Washington Post survey last year, only thirty-three percent of those asked believed in the Warren Commission's single shooter conclusion. What do you think, sir?"

Connally was pensive. "Hell's fire, Burke. Anyone with half a brain can figure
that there had to be at least one other shooter. The shot that hit me was fired too
close to the first shot to have come from that blunderbuss relic of a weapon Oswald
had. Had ta' be another shooter."

"John," his wife interrupted, "I think you've done quite enough for this afternoon. It's time for you to rest. You will excuse us, Mr. Burke?"

"Yes, ma'am. Thank you for seeing me."

SILVER SPRING, MARYLAND

"Hi there," Mike gushed to his wife, Marilyn.

"Hi there yourself," she replied. "What's going on in Dallas?"

"I've had some interesting interviews. Today I was in Austin visiting with Governor and Mrs. Connally."

"How were they?"

"Mrs. Connally is a real peach. You'd like her. The Governor got a little hot once or twice. But I accomplished what I was after. Actually, they were both most welcoming."

Marilyn got in a humorous dig. "Are all those Texas belles welcoming, too?"

"I wouldn't know, sweetheart. Aside from my visit to the Connallys, I haven't been out and about. Besides, I value my spot in bed next to you too much to bother looking."

"Just keep it that way, Buster," Marilyn demanded. "Want to talk with the kids?"

"You bet!" Mike responded quickly. "That's why I called before eight o'clock."

It wasn't but a couple of minutes before one of his daughters was on the phone.

"Hi, Dad," Ann greeted. "I miss you. When are you coming home?"

Why am I not surprised that Ann beat her sisters to the phone?

"I miss you too, little lady. I'll be home next weekend. How is the summer craft camp going?"

"Fine. We walk to camp with the new neighbor children," Ann informed him. "There are three boys. Mom told me that one of the boys is about my age. His name is David. I don't like him very much."

"Why not?"

"At the craft camp, he mussed up a finger painting I was trying to finish for you. I think he's nasty."

"Remember, Ann," Mike counseled his daughter. "He's new to the neighborhood, so be kind."

"I'll try."

"Good girl," Mike assured her. "Can I talk with your sisters?"

"Sure," Ann told him. "Susan is right here."

"Hi, Dad." his eldest daughter said.

"I miss you, sweetheart," Mike told her right off.

"Miss you too, Dad," Susan responded.

"I hear we have new neighbors."

"Yes. They moved into the house right across the street. They have three boys. One of them will be in my grade next year. His name is Robert. He doesn't talk much, but he seems nice."

"Ann told me one of the boys could be a problem."

"He already is, Dad. He is not nice at all. At camp today, he was always cutting into the line of kids waiting to get on the slide and tripping kids and pushing them down. He doesn't know how to play with others at all."

"Other than that, is camp fun?"

"Oh, yes, Dad. It is," Susan said with enthusiasm. "We did finger painting today. Tomorrow we finish making our newspaper bowls."

"What in heaven's name is a newspaper bowl?"

"Didn't you ever make one when you were a little boy?"

"Nope. I never even heard of one."

"I guess you never went to craft camp, then. Well, first, you turn a cereal bowl upside down. Then you take strips of newspaper soaked in a white paste and put them over the bowl; first one way, then the other. After you let it dry, you paint it, trim the edges and take it home. That's what we're going to do tomorrow."

"What would you use it for?"

"Mom asked the same question," Susan told him. "I told her that I'm going to use mine to hold my bobby pins and barrettes. Ann said she wanted hers for our popcorn nights. I don't know what Jackie will do with hers."

"Sounds good to me," Mike told her. "Is Jackie still awake?"

"Sorry, Dad," Susan told him. "She missed her nap this afternoon. So she was practically falling asleep during supper. Mom put her to bed right after our bath."

"Please tell her that I miss her. I'll call you guys around supper time in a couple of days, OK?"

"OK. Here's Mom. I love you."

"Thank you, sweetheart. I love you, too."

Marilyn took the phone. "Hi there."

"So we have some new neighbors?"

"Yup. Bob and Julie Miles moved into the old Burns house. I talked with her at craft camp this morning. They are native Marylanders. Bob Miles works for some company in D.C. She is a substitute teacher like me and is raising three kids, all boys. She seems nice."

"Super. We can use good neighbors our age. I hope the girls get along with their boys."

"Me too."

"Hey!" Mike asked. "Do you miss me yet?"

"Funny you should ask. Just this evening, I was on my knees by the tub giving the kids their bath and getting all soaked in the process. And it came to me. I miss you doing the bath thing, for sure."

"Oh, me," Mike moaned. "Thanks a lot. Is that all you miss?"

"Actually, I really miss you putting your arms around me and doing all the other stuff that usually follows."

"Good to hear, sweetheart," Mike responded. "I miss that, too."

"You just stay away from places like Jack Ruby's strip club. Promise?"

"Yes, dear. Of course, I promise. I assure you that I will suffer the pains of celibacy until the next time I'm within hugging distance of you; at least until the kids are in bed asleep."

"You better," Marilyn ordered. "I love you and truly miss you."

"Love you, too," Mike assured his wife. "Talk to you later this week."

***

"The question that suggests itself is: How could the President have been shot in the front from the back?"

— Richard Dudman: *St. Louis Post Dispatch*. December 1, 1963.

PARKLAND MEMORIAL HOSPITAL, DALLAS, TEXAS

First thing Monday morning, Harold Ryan had an appointment with Dr. Kent Clark.

"Good morning, Doctor," Harold began. "It's good of you to meet with me."

"It's quite all right, Mr. Ryan; I'm happy to help in any way I can. I do have a class at nine this morning. If your business with me takes longer, we'll have to meet again later."

"That's fine, Doctor. If we can take care of some preliminaries first, we'll get right to my questions."

"Fine."

"On November 22, 1963, you were chairman of the Department of Neurosurgery at Parkland Hospital?"

"Yes, I was. Still am, as a matter of fact."

"I'm told that you are so intense in the operating room that some medical people call you, The Cobra. Is that true, Doctor?"

"I've heard rumors to that effect, Mr. Ryan. You see, an operating room is much like a battlefield. Those present are fighting a battle for the life of a patient. I have little patience with timid people in that arena. I've been known to be short-tempered with such people and even kick them out of the battle scene."

"I've read an article written by Tom Wicker published in the *New York Times* on November 22, 1963. He quotes you as saying that when you first saw President Kennedy in the ER, you had concluded immediately that he could not live. Is that an accurate quote, Doctor?"

"Yes, it is," Kent responded. "Working in the ER as often as I have, you get to recognize such things. I certainly always work for a different outcome, though."

"Other than that, what else did you observe when you entered Trauma Room #1 on November 22nd?"

"I saw several doctors administering emergency treatment to President Kennedy.

"Doctor Ceracco was putting a tube into the throat of the president while Dr. Perry was examining a wound at the throat. Drs. Baxter and Crenshaw were administering fluids and blood. Other medical personnel were assisting. When it became apparent that the president was not getting enough air down the tube in his throat, Dr. Perry made an incision at the site of the throat wound to complete a tracheostomy. It was apparent that the President had sustained a lethal wound," Kent explained, "A missile had gone in and out of the back of his head, causing external lacerations and loss of brain tissue."

At this point, Ryan interrupted.

"You are quoted as saying, 'My God, the whole right side of his head is shot off. We've nothing to work with.' Is that true, Doctor?"

"Most likely, I did. There was blood and brain matter spattered all over people in the room and on the table. The head wound was massive. A good third of his brain was lying on the table, too. So I probably said something like that."

"Doctor," Ryan asked. "Do you have any thoughts about the directionality of the shots that caused such damage to the president's head?"

"At the time, I was only concerned with saving President Kennedy's life. So I did not dwell on that question."

"And, since?" Ryan continued.

"Mr. Ryan," Clark began. "I have worked on patients in the Parkland emergency room many times, thousands probably. So when I see a head wound as massive as his, I would assume that the projectile which caused it to have entered from the front."

"What else do you remember before you declared President Kennedy dead?"

"I tried to find a carotid pulse and failed," Kent continued, "Medically, it was apparent the president was not alive when he was brought in. There was no spontaneous respiration. He had dilated, fixed pupils. It was obvious he had a lethal head wound. So Dr. Perry began closed-chest cardiac massage. I relieved him after a bit. But when a pulse could still not be found, it was decided to pronounce the president dead. Then, I remember saying, 'There's nothing more to be done.'"

"Why did you fix the time of death at one o'clock?"

"That was an approximate time, Mr. Ryan. It's not unusual for us to do that in trauma room cases. We get so busy just trying to save the patient's life we often pay no attention to the time. On November 22nd, I assure you, no one was monitoring the clock; all of us were too busy trying to save the president's life. But when it became obvious that we could not do so, I looked at my watch and chose one o'clock."

"Thank you for your time, Doctor," Ryan said. "May I contact you should another question come up?"

"Certainly, Mr. Ryan."

***

His next appointment was with Dr. Crenshaw.

After the preliminaries were completed, Ryan went right to the central question.

"When a patient is brought to the trauma room, Doctor, what is the standard care procedure?"

"We call it the ABCs of trauma care: A is airway, B is breathing, C stands for circulation."

"And, this was the procedure followed that day?"

"Yes. Would you like me to take you through everything done on November 22nd for President Kennedy, Mr. Ryan?"

"Yes, please do."

"Because the bullet that had entered his neck had pierced his windpipe, Dr. Carrico had forced an endotracheal tube down Kennedy's throat for breathing. The trauma room nurses stripped the president of his shoes and clothing, except for his undershorts. Then I began the insertion of a plastic tube in the vein of the left leg to give a rapid infusion of fluids. Dr. Curtis began a similar procedure on the right leg. It was decided that the tube that had been placed down the president's throat was not sufficient, so Dr. Perry decided to perform a tracheotomy on the president's throat. He chose to enlarge the existing wound where a bullet had entered the neck between the second and third tracheal cartilages. Doctors McClelland and Baxter helped him. Moments later, Drs. Baxter and Peters began inserting an anterior chest tube on the president's right side, and Drs. Jones and McClelland did the same thing on the left side to further assist in his breathing by expanding the chest cavity. By this time, President Kennedy had been in the room for about twenty minutes. A tracheotomy had been performed. He was on an automatic breathing machine; tubes had been inserted into his chest to get air into his lungs, and his circulation had been improved by the cut-downs in his legs. We had fluids, O-negative blood, and Ringer's lactate flowing through the enlarged portals into one arm and both legs. The ABCs of trauma care had been completed."

"Had the president been declared dead yet, doctor?"

"No, he hadn't," Dr. Crenshaw recalled. "But I've got to tell you, Mr. Ryan, I walked to the head of the table to get a closer look at the president's head. His right cerebral hemisphere appeared to be gone. It looked like a crater – an empty cavity. Using emergency room standards, I saw it as a four-plus injury, which no one survives. Dr. Jenkins hooked up a machine that measures heartbeat. When it was switched on, the green light moved across the screen in a straight line without giving even a hint of the slightest cardiac activity."

Dr. Crenshaw concluded. "Dr. Perry, bless his heart, just wouldn't give up. He began closed-chest cardiac massage. Dr. Jenkins continued to administer pure oxygen. When Dr. Perry tired, Dr. Kent took his place. None of us wanted to quit. A cardiopathy scope was attached. Again, the straight green light traversed the scope. Dr. Jenkins reached over and closed the valve to the anesthesia machine. We had just witnessed the most tragic event imaginable, the president's death."

"Phew! That's quite a description, Doctor."

"I don't think any of us will ever forget it, Mr. Ryan."

"Doctor," Ryan began. "You mentioned that Dr. Perry enlarged the wound that entered the President's throat to perform a tracheotomy."

"Yes, that's right."

"Can you describe that wound?"

"It was an entrance wound the size of a pencil eraser."

"You're sure it was not an exit wound, Doctor?"

"We treat patients with bullet wounds in the emergency room all the time, Mr. Ryan. I've seen and treated hundreds of them. I know an entrance wound when I see one."

"That's what Dr. Perry said at a press conference held later on November 22nd."

"What about the head wound, Doctor?" Ryan pressed. "Do you have any thoughts about the directionality of the bullet that caused that wound?"

"Based upon my close observation of the president's head wound and my experience with gunshot wound treatment in Parkland Hospital, I would say it came from the front, just like the throat wound."

Standing, Ryan said, "Thank you for your time, Doctor. You have been most helpful."

***

That evening over supper, Mike had a suggestion.

"Harold," he began. "How about taking in a movie tonight?"

"What are you talking about, Mike?" Harold chuckled. We've both had a long day and look forward to an early start tomorrow. I think I'll pass."

"The film runs for less than ten minutes."

"This sounds fishy. You've got something up your sleeve, Burke. What is it?"

"Zapruder invited us over to watch the uncut version of his film of the Kennedy assassination. You know, the one Time-Life bought from him. Want ta' go with me to see it?"

"Smart ass," Ryan snorted. "Is the Pope Catholic?"

"Well, you had better finish that piece of pie and drink your coffee because we're due at his place in fifteen minutes."

"You are sure full of surprises, Burke."

"Handsome, too, Ryan. Don't leave that out."

By the time they found the Zapruder residence, they were a few minutes late.

"Welcome to our home," Mrs. Zapruder told them. "Can I get you some coffee or a soft drink?"

Both men declined.

"We just finished supper, ma'am," Ryan told her.

"I believe we're fine, thank you," Burke said.

"My husband has the screen set up in our recreation room. Please follow me." After introductions, Mr. Zapruder ran the film.

"Could you please run it again, sir?" Ryan asked.

"Certainly," Zapruder told him.

Again and again, the three men watched the tragedy unfold on the screen.

"Phew!" Burke exclaimed. "Watching the head shot sure gets to you."

"Mr. Zapruder," Ryan asked. "Let me ask your opinion about the shot your film shows hitting the president's head. Do you think that shot came from the front or the back?"

"I believe my film makes it very clear that shot came from the front of the president. In fact, I told the Warren Commission people that I thought at least one shot came from behind where I was standing and filming on the Grassy Knoll."

"Thank you for your hospitality, sir," Burke said, shaking his host's hand.

"Please give our thanks to Mrs. Zapruder too, sir."

"I will, gentlemen," Zapruder responded. "My wife left the room before I ran the film. She won't watch the film anymore. It upsets her too much."

"I can understand that." Ryan agreed.

The two men rode to their motel in silence.

"How about we compare notes on the film tomorrow over supper?" Burke suggested.

"That sounds good to me. See you tomorrow."

FEDERAL BUREAU OF INVESTIGATION

At the conclusion of one of their routine meetings, Director Hoover asked his deputy, William Sullivan, to stay for a moment.

When everyone else had left his office, Hoover asked,

"What's happening with your boy, Burke?"

Now, Burke is 'my' boy. The boss does this all the time. Why am I not surprised?

"He's in Dallas with Ryan this week, interviewing a long list of people. I've given him a conference room to use. Conversations in the room are being taped, so I'll have a transcript of all the interviews conducted there. I also have a list of all the appointments they've made."

"Anything to worry about, Bill?"

"They're just going over old ground, sir," Sullivan responded. "I don't think there's anything new there for them to discover."

Hoover wondered, "I'd hate to read the papers one morning that something new or sensational has been turned up by these two."

"Of course, sir." Sullivan agreed.

"As I recall, Burke's wife successfully put pressure on him to leave us several years ago. It was a good word from you that got him his current position on the Hill. I wonder if she can still influence him. Let's see. Possibly, she can discover that her husband has a firm offer from a Maryland or D.C. firm. Tell her this firm needs a good family man with his qualifications and experience to fill a position right now. Do you think that's a possibility, Bill?" Hoover asked.

"I believe it can be arranged, sir."

"Let me know in a day or two, tops."

"Yes, sir."

LIFE MAGAZINE OCTOBER 2, 1964

Congressman Gerald R. Ford: Warren Commission Member: "After taking millions of words of testimony from hundreds upon hundreds of witnesses, the Warren Commission has established that there is not a scintilla of credible evidence to suggest a conspiracy to kill President Kennedy. The evidence is clear and overwhelming; Lee Harvey Oswald did it."

DALLAS, TEXAS

Burke was on the phone with Jesse Curry.

"Mr. Burke," the retired Chief of the Dallas Police Department began. "You're staying at the new Howard Johnson's right by the expressway?"

"That's right, Chief."

"Let's meet for breakfast in their restaurant instead of the FBI headquarters, all right?"

"If you want to, Chief. Is eight o'clock too early for you?"

"Naw," he responded. "I'm up an' wandering around the house by six. How does seven o'clock suit ya'?"

"That'll be fine. I'll have a cup of hot coffee waiting for ya' at seven tomorrow morning."

"See ya' then, Burke."

***

Burke watched as a tall, heavy-set fella entered the Howard Johnson restaurant from the street. It only seemed to take the man a minute to spot him.

"Mornin' Burke," he said. "See you got my coffee poured."

"How'd you know it was me, Chief?"

"I jus' looked for a table with a man dressed in a suit an' tie who had two cups of coffee in front of him."

"Good guess?"

"Not hardly, Burke. Remember, I was the Chief of Police."

"Why did you want to meet here instead of the FBI office?"

Curry took a sip of his coffee, eyeing Mike at the same time.

"You FBI, Burke?"

"I spent four years with them. I've been working as a staffer with the House Judiciary Committee the last six years."

"Ya'? Well, I'll tell ya anyway," Curry said, setting his cup on the table and looking into Mike's eyes. "I don't trust those sons-a-bitches. ' Sides, what's worse, they're arrogant sons-a-bastards, every one."

"Why don't you really tell me what you think of the fine men of the Bureau?" Burke chuckled.

"Don't get me started unloading, Burke."

"Not at all, Chief," Burke assured him. "Why in hell do you think I'm here in Dallas paying for all this fine coffee? I want you to unload. I need someone to unload. Secrets have been kept long enough. It's about time we all spoke freely, don't you think?"

Curry chuckled.

"Not in an FBI conference room that's probably bugged."

"I expect that's true, Chief," Mike admitted. "All right, we're not in that room now. It's just you, me, and my tape recorder."

"What happens to that tape you're making when we leave here, mister former FBI agent?"

"You get it back in the mail from me."

"Copies?"

"You got my word, no copies. I'll take notes and maybe even quote you in my final report. But no copies will be made of the tape."

"Your word?"

"You got it, Chief," Burke said again. "No copies will be made."

"All right, young fella, I'll trust you on that. But you're right. It is about time for some fresh air in the room. What do you want to know?"

"Did Oswald do it, Chief?"

"We don't have any proof that Oswald fired the rifle and never did. Nobody's been able to put him in that building with a gun in his hand. There was evidence that he might have killed Officer Tippit, though."

"I've read that your people had a paraffin test for nitrates done on Oswald."

"Yes, we did. There was evidence on his hands that he had fired a pistol. But there was no evidence on his cheek that he had fired a rifle."

"How likely is that?" Burke asked. "If he had actually had fired a rifle?"

"Not likely at all, young fella'; probably not even possible."

"Didn't anyone see him at the Book Depository Building around the time of the shooting?"

"Yes. Carolyn Arnold gave a statement that she saw Oswald on the first floor at about 12:25. That would make it pretty tough for him to be at the sixth-floor window ready to go as the parade vehicles made the turn onto Elm Street. Then, one of my officers swore that he entered the Book Depository Building to investigate less than two minutes after the shooting. He was joined by the superintendent of the Book Depository as he ran up the stairway from the ground floor. They both saw Oswald on the second-floor level, sitting at a table, having a Coke, and reading a paper. "According to their statements, they saw him less than a minute, two at the most, of the shooting."

"Couldn't Oswald have just run down from the sixth floor?"

"Not likely. The rifle was found by the sheriff's people fully loaded and hidden behind some boxes near the sixth-floor stairway. So after firing three shots, Oswald would have had to take the time to reload the rifle and then hide it. Then he would have had to sprint down from the sixth floor to be seen casually drinking a soda and reading a newspaper on the second floor, all in less than sixty to ninety seconds. I don't think so. Besides, there were two female employees using the stairway at the time. Neither of them reported Oswald on that stairway. Did he fly down to the second floor?"

"Back then, the word around D.C. was that local security for the Dallas motorcade was lax, almost nonexistent. What do you have to say about that?"

"That kind a' talk back then really pissed me off, Burke, still does." Curry spat. "The implication, a' course, is that Kennedy's death was our fault. Look. The Dallas Police don't live in a vacuum. We were aware of how our counterparts in Nashville, Germany, New York, and Paris covered the visit of the president and First Lady. They had the place covered with security on those visits. We knew that parades in Chicago and Miami had been canceled because of credible assassination threats. The Tampa visit had been severely modified, as well. So when he comes to Dallas, what is different? The warnings were there. Law enforcement people talk to one another. We were in contact with folks from Chicago, Miami, and Tampa. If we had to have that parade, why were so few of our people used? We had a lot a' people just standing around, Burke. For example, I could have assigned many more men to the buildings like they did for the Nashville visit. None of the feds asked our opinion about the security problems involved in a parade route using Elm Street. My Lord, Burke, jus' think of it! As our vehicles made that turn from Houston onto Elm Street, all the cars had to slow down. We were barely moving at a crawl. With the tall buildings on each side, an' windows not ordered shut, the Book Depository behind, the Grassy Knoll on the right, and the underpass directly ahead, Elm Street was a shooter's wet dream. Ask the Sheriff. Before the visit, he and I talked. We usually share information, and we give each other a hand from time to time. He had so many extra men, probably near a hundred, he gave many of them permission to watch the parade. They could have just as easily been part of the security."

"Why weren't they?"

"You'll have to ask the Secret Service guys that question."

"I will."

"The guys you should really ask about the poor security are Wes Larson and Forrest Sorrels. Larson was in charge of the Secret Service detail for the Dallas visit. Sorrels was in charge of the Dallas Secret Service office and was officially Larson's boss. Larson sat in my vehicle during the parade with his boss, bitching the whole time about how short he was of Secret Service agents, an' all. He also complained about how the whirlwind trip with so many stops in just a few days had exhausted his agents, too. It was enough to bring a fella' to tears."

"Why weren't you sympathetic, Chief?"

"His moaning fell on deaf ears because the Sheriff and I knew that nine of the agents in his detail had been out the night before drinkin' in Fort Worth, illegally, at an after-hours private club called the Cellar Door. They were out until after three that very morning. Nine a' them were members of the detail responsible for the protection of President Kennedy. Seven of 'em were still there at 3:30 AM. When they knew they had to report for duty at Love Field at 8:00 AM. They even joked about how they left a couple a' local firemen guarding the president and Mrs. Kennedy's hotel room."

"How did you know all that, Chief?"

"I'm supposed ta' know such things, Burke." He responded. "Actually though, Mike Schieffer, who's the night police reporter for the Fort Worth *Star-Telegram*, told me. He was there to see the sun come up with seven members of the Kennedy detail. On top a' that, we were ready to help with manpower. But Larson never asked. In fact, at the Secret Service security briefing held on November 21st, they canceled one of my police cars full of deputies. Larsen re-assigned my people to guard the podium at the luncheon site. I was concerned as all hell and complained about it. He said his people had the parade covered. Was this just their arrogance, ya' think, Burke? Did they think so little of us? Or, maybe they wanted the president exposed like he was. We heard later that the security folks at the air force base volunteered as many security men as needed to help secure the Texas visit. But for all Larsen's complaining, he only took about fifty a' them. An' remember, Burke, we knew that the president's advance people objected to using Elm Street on the basis that it was a more difficult route to secure than the regular parade route on Main Street. Kennedy's advance people also brought up the fact that the sharp right turn required to get onto Houston Street and then again the left turn onto Elm forced the president's car to slow down to an unacceptable speed, which by the way, was against the protocol of the Secret Service. Just tha' same, the Secret Service guys in Dallas stepped in and settled the argument by approving the Elm

Street route. They said it would not be a security problem. They insisted that they had it covered. Burke, it was as though Larsen and his Secret Service people were setting President Kennedy up."

"Chief," Burke changed the subject. "You are quoted as saying you thought one or more shots came from the front of the motorcade. Were you quoted correctly?"

"Yes, I was," Curry admitted. "I was always good for a statement for the local press. Right after the shooting, they asked me for an opinion, so I told 'em that I believed at least one shot came from in front of the limo, maybe two. The Sheriff and I are old hands at police work, Burke. Over the years, most law enforcement officers develop a sense of direction when they hear a shot. So when ya' do hear a shot, experienced police officers like us instinctively look that way. The Sheriff and I both looked front-right after the first shot, toward the Grassy Knoll. He even got on his radio and sent some of his deputies over there to investigate a puff of smoke he had seen when he looked in that direction. As I recall, a few doctors at Parkland Hospital held a press conference right after Kennedy was declared dead. At that conference, I believe more than one doctor said that Kennedy's throat wound was an entry wound. That means a bullet struck the president from the front, not the back."

"Yes, they did say that, Chief," Burke agreed. "Have you changed your mind about any of that?" he asked.

'Not a 'tall. The Feds leaned on me a bit back then after they decided that all the shots had to come from behind. The Sheriff caved some, but I never did. Don't see any reason to now, neither."

"If anything comes up, can I contact you again, Chief?"

"Sure thing, Mr. Burke," he responded. "But I expect to hear from you again when you allow me to read about this interview in your report before you submit it. Won't I?"

Burke smiled. "Of course, Chief. We'll talk then, for sure."

***

Burke hurried over to the conference room at the FBI office for his ten o'clock interview with Dallas Patrolman Joe Marshall Smith.

On his way to the conference room, Burke met Smith in the hallway.

"Patrolman Smith," he said, extending his hand in greeting. "Thank you so much for coming."

"Happy to, Mr. Burke. I'm due to report for my shift soon, so I only have a few minutes."

"Great. Let's go into the room and get started."

The preliminaries were quickly completed, and Burke asked his first question.

"I understand you were on duty directing traffic at the corner of Elm and Houston as the president's motorcade passed. Is that true?"

"Yes, sir, I was."

"As soon as the motorcade passed onto Elm, what happened?"

"Shots rang out, that's what," Smith stated. "I looked in the direction of where I thought a gun had gone off."

"In what direction did you look?"

"I looked toward the fence on the Grassy Knoll to my right. Then this woman came up to me all hysterical and screamed, 'They're shooting at the president from the bushes!' So I immediately proceed up there. I took off running in the direction she had pointed, the Grassy Knoll, ya' know. When I got close to the fence, I was ordered to stop by a man in a suit."

"And?"

"He flashed ID; said he was Secret Service and I was to return to my post, back on Elm and Houston."

"What did you do, then?"

"I did as he told me. Later, I informed my supervisor of what I had seen."

"Anything else, Patrolman?"

"That's about it, Mr. Burke," Smith responded. "Do you have any more questions?"

Burke stood and extended his hand.

"No, I don't. The information you have given me will be most helpful. I'll let you go. You can report for your shift. Thank you for your time."

***

Police Sgt. D.V. Harkness was next.

"Good morning, Sergeant. I'm Michael Burke. Thank you for coming."

"You're most welcome, Mr. Burke," Harkness responded. "How can I help your investigation?"

"You can tell me what you witnessed on November 22, 1963."

"It was a madhouse along President Kennedy's parade route that day. The crowd was bigger than we had anticipated. I was supervising my officers, who were directing traffic and dealing with the crowd. As soon as a shot rang out, I turned in that direction and started running toward it."

"In what direction was that, Sergeant?"

"I ran toward the wooden fence to the right of the intersection of Elm and Houston; the fence on the Grassy Knoll."

"What did you see there?"

"I saw several men in suits. I also saw that there was a rifle held by one of the men. One of the men ordered me away. He told me they were Secret Service."

"So what did you do?"

"I went away like he told me."

***

It was 11:30, and Ed Hoffman arrived right on time for his appointment.

"Good morning, Mr. Hoffman," Burke began. "Thank you for coming."

"My boss let me out a bit early for lunch. But I have to be back by 12:30. I hope that will give us enough time."

"Well then," Burke said. "We had better move along. I understand, Mr. Hoffman, that you saw a man aim and fire a rifle toward the approaching motorcade. Is that true?"

"Yes. That's true. I couldn't believe my eyes. I focused on a gentleman wearing a suit and a hat at the picket fence. Then, I saw a puff of smoke and a man with a rifle."

"From where exactly did he fire?"

"He was behind the wooden fence on the Grassy Knoll."

"Did you see anything else?"

"Yes. After he had fired one shot, he walked down the railroad embankment and gave the rifle to another man. That man placed it in a car, got in, and drove away."

"Anything else?"

"Not really. But given what happened to the president, isn't that enough?"

"It certainly is, Mr. Hoffman. It is quite enough. Thank you for taking the time to tell me what you saw that terrible day."

"You're welcome, Mr. Burke."

***

After lunch, Burke's first interview was with James Tague.

Burke stood to greet Mr. Tague. "Good afternoon," he said, extending his hand. "Thank you for coming."

"I wouldn't miss this opportunity to tell my story, Mr. Burke."

"I'm sorry it took so long for your story to be recognized as important enough to hear."

"Right," Tague responded with a chuckle. "As my wife tells people, I'm the third person wounded at Dealey Plaza on November 22, 1963."

"That is, in fact, correct, isn't it?" Burke responded. "Tell me about it, please."

"Well, I was standing near the entrance to the triple underpass looking down Elm Street and saw the president's motorcade turn left onto Elm and move toward me and the underpass. Suddenly, I heard shots coming from my left, the Grassy Knoll. Just as suddenly, I was struck on the cheek by a sharp piece of concrete. I approached the first police officer I saw, a Sheriff's Deputy Eddy Walthers, and told him I had been hit by a piece of concrete or something. He saw the cut on my face, examined the curb, and confirmed that something had hit it, as I had said. That afternoon, I called the Dallas FBI and told them about the bullet striking the curb and a piece of it hitting me. They thanked me for the information. I never heard back from them. In the *Dallas Morning Times* of December 5, 1964, I read that the FBI had decided that there were three shots fired, as proven by three shell casings they found on the sixth floor of the Depository. In light of that decision, I can see why my fourth bullet would have been difficult for them to explain. I had gone back to the site in May of that year to find the mark on the cement curb where I believed a bullet had hit. Only faint traces of the bullet mark were still there. Anyway, on July 23rd, a member of the Warren Commission staff, a guy named Wesley Liebler, interviewed me. I told him the same story I told you."

"Well," Burke began. "Let me fill you in, Mr. Tague."

"It appears that Dallas Assistant US attorney Martha Joe Stroud sent a letter to Lee Rankin of the Warren Commission on June 9, 1964. She reported your incident and the fact that a Dallas reporter, Tom Dillard, had photographed the pavement showing what looked like a piece of lead had struck it. The Warren Commission couldn't ignore this. So, on July 17, they asked the FBI to look into it. The reply was that there was no mark observed on the curb. Despite this, the Commission felt it couldn't ignore a Dallas policeman's report, a sheriff's deputy's report, and a letter from a U.S. assistant prosecutor. As a result, you were finally questioned in Dallas by one of the Commission's attorneys, Liebler. After you gave your testimony, the Commission again asked the FBI to look into the matter. This time they found the mark, removed that piece of curb, and took it to Washington for analysis. In an August 12, 1964 response to the Commission, the FBI acknowledged that the mark on the curb had been made by the lead from a rifle bullet."

"So, I'm right after all?" Tague said.

"It would seem so." Burke agreed.

Tague surmised. "Seems ta' me that means there was actually a fourth shot fired that day, doesn't it? Let me see if I have this correct. One bullet hit the curb to launch the chip that hit me; another bullet went through the limo's windshield; the bullet that hit the president's head and killed him would be a third. The fourth bullet would be the so-called 'magic bullet' that the Commission said went through the president's back and into the governor."

"It might interest you to know, Mr. Tague," Burke said, smiling, "Dallas County Sheriff Decker, who was riding in the lead car, saw what he thinks was a bullet striking the pavement when he turned in response to the first shot fired. What he saw was verified by a motorcycle officer named Chaney, who reported seeing the same thing. So it would seem that five shots were fired that day, not just four."

"But the FBI said there were only three shots fired, Mr. Burke."

"Curious, isn't it, Mr. Tague?"

***

Burke's next interview was with Bill and Gayle Newman.

"We were in Dealey Plaza with our two sons to see President Kennedy. We had missed seeing him and Mrs. Kennedy at Love Field. We wanted our sons to see them. So we hurried downtown to catch the parade. We found a spot on Elm Street in front of the concrete cupola on the Grassy Knoll. Shortly after the president's limo made the turn onto Elm, I heard two shots real close together. I could see the president's face real clearly. He looked shocked. When the limo got closer, I saw the side of his head just blow off, and he was knocked violently back. My wife and I were looking right at the president when the shots came from behind us. I shouted for my wife and kids to lie down."

"Were you and the kids all right, Mrs. Newman?

"We were pretty shaken, believe me," she confessed.

"What happened next?"

Gayle continued. "A reporter from TV Channel 8 interviewed us and then took us to the TV station to record our statement again. Sheriff Deputies were waiting for us there. They took us to their headquarters and questioned us there for several hours. It was tough on the kids."

"Did anyone from the federal government contact you?"

"Yes, Mr. Burke, FBI agents came to our house on Sunday, November 24, 1963."

"What did they want?"

"They asked us the same questions we answered at the Dallas Sheriff's office."

Gayle Newman added, "Since that time, you are the first to ask us what we saw."

"Do you have anything more to add?" Burke asked.

"I have a question, Mr. Burke," Gayle said.

"What is that, Mrs. Newman?"

"How can the FBI and the Warren Commission people insist that all the shots fired that day in Dallas came from behind President Kennedy? she asked.

"A very large number of Americans have been asking the same question, Mrs. Newman. That's why I'm here in Dallas talking with witnesses like you."

The interview over, Bill Newman stood but commented as he left the room.

"I hope you get to the bottom of it, Mr. Burke. For our government to cover up the assassination with those two reports is awful. It's a damn shame."

***

Dolores Kounas was standing on the south side of Elm Street, opposite the Texas School Book Depository Building.

"Thank you for taking your lunch break to talk with me today, Ms. Kounas."

"Dolores, please, Mr. Burke," she urged.

"All right, Dolores. What did you see and hear that day back on November 22, 1963?"

"Something I never even imagined I'd see, ever; that's for sure," she said. "I'd taken my lunch break that day too. As the motorcade passed where I was standing, I heard a shot, then two more ring out."

"Where did you think they came from?"

"I did not look up at the buildings as I had thought the shots came from a westerly direction in the vicinity of the viaduct."

"I see you gave that same testimony to the Warren Commission back in March of 1964."

"That's right, I did," Dolores replied, "But it seems that they decided I was mistaken. Nevertheless, Mr. Burke, I know what I heard. A person doesn't forget something as terrible as that. Besides, I'm not deaf yet."

***

Burke was scheduled to interview Roy Truly, the director and superintendent of the Texas School Book Depository on November 22, 1963.

"Good afternoon, sir," Mike greeted him. "It's good of you to come."

"Anything I can do to help, Mr. Burke."

As the motorcade passed his building, he was standing with Ochus Campbell on the north side of Elm Street, close to the TSBD building.

"Where did you think the shots came from, Mr. Truly?" Mike asked.

"A lawyer from the Warren Commission asked me that back in March of 1964. I told him then that I thought the shots came from the vicinity of the railroad or the WPA project (the concrete structure), behind the WPA project west of the building."

"I also understand you told Sherriff Decker that you saw Oswald sitting in a second-floor lunch room reading a paper right after the shooting. That right?"

"Sure did," Truly responded, "I surely don't know if he killed Mr. Kennedy, but ya know something, Mr. Burke? It be mighty hard for most anybody to put another shell in the chamber a' that rifle, hide the gun behind some boxes, and get down four flights of stairs in not much more than a minute.

"If that weren't enough, after killing the President of the United States, Oswald was also sposed ta' get a cola outta our machine and then sit there calm as you please reading a paper. I didn't know the fella well, ya' see. But it jus' seems hard to believe he could do all that in less than 90 seconds. I know I couldn't. Could you, Mr. Burke?"

"The FBI and the Warren Commission believed he did it, Mr. Truly."

"Ya, they did, Mr. Burke. But them's the same bunch who thought only three bullets were fired, too."

***

Burke's next interview wasn't until 3:30. He had scheduled his interview that late because the man he wanted to talk with had a work conflict. Actually, he welcomed the chance to get some paperwork in order.

Right on time, motorcycle Patrolman Bobby W. Hargis knocked on the conference room door.

"Mr. Burke?" Hargis asked. "I have an appointment with you?"

"Yes, you do, Mr. Hargis. Thank you for being so prompt."

"Quite all right, sir. Anything I can do to help."

After Burke had gotten Hargis a cup of coffee and himself a refill, he began the interview.

"Officer Hargis," he began. "Why did you follow the president's vehicle instead of traveling alongside as was the typical arrangement?"

"Well, sir," Hargis replied. "It was the strangest thing. Patrolman Baker and I were assigned to do just that; travel alongside the president's limo, that is. But when we arrived at Love Field at 8 a.m., the Secret Service told us not to do that. Something to do with President Kennedy's wish to let the crowd see him better.

We were told to fall back and follow his vehicle instead. So, I followed to the left and rear of his limo."

"Who gave you those instructions?"

"The Secret Service guy who was in charge gave the orders."

"Was his name Wes Larson?"

"I think so."

"You testified to the Warren Commission that after the fatal head shot, you were hit by a spray of blood and other body material. Tell me about that."

"People from the Warren Commission interviewed me and Baker. They asked us about what we heard and what we saw. They weren't too interested in the spray that hit me and my bike, though."

"What gave you that impression?"

"I say that because the guy conducting the interview never asked about that. I just volunteered the information."

"What did you tell him?"

"I told him that at one point, the windshield of my bike, my helmet, and the right shoulder of my uniform were sprayed with blood, pieces of flesh, and other stuff. I still dream a' that part. Cleaning it off my bike was something I never want to do again. Pretty gruesome being it was part of the president's head an' all."

"Were you asked what you thought about where the bullet came from?"

"You mean the direction it came from?"

"Yes."

"No, I wasn't. But it had to come from ahead a' me some. If it had come from behind, the people in front of President Kennedy would have gotten sprayed instead, seems ta me."

"It seems like, to a lot of people, Mr. Hargis. Do you remember anything else?"

"I'll never forget as long as I live, the sight of Mrs. Kennedy crawling a' top the trunk to retrieve a piece a' the president's head that landed there. The whole thing haunts me, Mr. Burke."

"It haunts a lot of people, patrolman," Burke assured him. "I think that's why I'm in Dallas talking with you."

"Can I ask you a question, Mr. Burke?"

"Sure. What is it?"

"If I'm right and the shot that hit President Kennedy's head came from the front, how come Oswald is blamed as the only shooter? He was behind the president."

Burke smiled and said, "Mr. Hargis, you have asked the very question that many Americans have been asking."

"It don't seem ta' me like he could a' been since he was supposed to be in the building that was behind the motorcade."

"Exactly, Mr. Hargis."

***

Over at Parkland Hospital, Harold Ryan was beginning his last interview of the day, as well.

Margaret Henchcliffe took a seat in the small office Ryan was using for his interviews.

"Thank you for giving me some of your time, Miss Henchcliffe."

"I'd be more comfortable if you would just call me Margaret, Mr. Ryan."

"As you wish, Margaret," he responded. "First, will you tell me how long you have been an emergency room nurse?"

"I've been a registered nurse for 15 years. The last eight years have been here at Parkland, mostly in the Emergency Room."

"You were on duty when President Kennedy was brought into the emergency room?"

"Yes, I was. I was not just on duty that day. I was actually in the trauma room where his body was treated."

"Will you describe the scene there after he was brought in?"

"It was chaos," she replied. "Dr. Carrico was the only doctor there at first. But the call went out for others, and the room soon filled with doctors. Not only were doctors coming in to treat the wounded president, but Secret Service agents crowded into the room, too. Even Mrs. Kennedy was standing near the table where her husband had been laid. It was a wonder the doctors could get anything done. One Secret Service agent was even running around the room with a drawn pistol. I went up to him and reminded him that there was no assassin in the room. I told him to leave the room and let us try to save the president's life. Then, he left the trauma room. I don't know what happened to him. He was acting real crazy."

"Margaret," Ryan began, "I have a list of doctors reported to be in the room treating the president. Would you please look at it? Is there any doctor on the list you do not remember being in the room that day?"

Margaret reviewed the list. She handed it back to Ryan and said, "No, Mr. Ryan, all the doctors you have on that list were there."

"Thank you."

"Did you assist Dr. Perry when he performed the tracheotomy?"

"Yes, I did. You have to understand, though, as a nurse, I take orders from doctors as they initiate procedures. I don't perform them. That day, another nurse, a Miss Brown, helped me take off the president's clothes. She and I obtained the tubing they used to pump nitrates and blood into his body and air into his lungs. Dr. Perry and those assisting him needed instruments to complete the procedure you mentioned. I handed what they needed to them. They did the procedure, the tracheotomy."

"Did you see the throat wound before it was enlarged by Dr. Perry during that procedure?"

"Oh yes, I did," Mrs. Henchcliffe said, "It was a wound not much bigger than a pencil's eraser."

"Do you think it was an entry wound, Margaret?"

"You aren't the first one to question my opinion about that, Mr. Ryan. That big shot from Washington, Mr. Specter, really leaned on me to change my recollection. He tried to shake me up some, too. His bully tactics didn't change the facts. I saw an entrance wound in the president's throat, pure an' simple. He let me alone after I reminded him that several of the doctors who treated President Kennedy gave a press conference later that day. At that time, they talked about seeing an entrance wound to the throat of the president, too."

"Yes, they did, Margaret," Harold confirmed.

"I've been doing emergency room work for a bunch a' years, Mr. Ryan. I help treat gunshot injuries all the time. I'm no rookie in this kind a' work. Ask any ER doctor. They'll tell you Margaret Henchcliffe knows her stuff. They want me by their side in tough situations, too. You ask 'em."

"That's what doctors have told me too, Margaret. I was not questioning your veracity or your honest recollection. Please forgive me if I gave that impression. Do you recall anything else about that day?"

"No, sir. Do you have any more questions?" she responded.

"No, Margaret. I think we've covered this very well."

"What they did to that poor man, right in front of his wife, is something I'll never forgive. And there she was, right in the trauma room, watching him lying there naked, an' us putting tubes into him, an' all. We see a lot of terrible stuff in the ER, Mr. Ryan. And I'm not a rookie in emergency room work. But I'll never get over what I saw and had to do that day. Why are people in Washington so afraid of the truth, Mr. Ryan?"

"Good question, Margaret," Ryan agreed.

***

Just as Ryan was getting ready to leave, he heard a knock on the door.

"Come in," he said.

A man who looked the part of a doctor entered.

"Excuse me, Mr. Ryan," he said. "I'm Doctor McClelland. My appointment is not until tomorrow, but I have a conflict and won't be able to make it. Could we talk now instead?"

"Certainly," Ryan assured him. "Have a seat.

Ryan got right to the point. "I've had an opportunity to talk with both Dr. Clark and Dr. Crenshaw. Could you describe the president's wounds?"

"I first observed the throat wound," McClellan began. "It was a small entry wound about the size of a pencil eraser. Two doctors used that opening to perform a tracheotomy procedure."

"I took a look at the head wound, too," he continued. "It was a massive cavity on the back of the head, what we would call a 4 Plus injury."

"Would that head injury result from a bullet hitting the front or the back of the head?"

"It was definitely an exit wound, Mr. Ryan," Dr. McClellan said. "To cause that type of exit wound, the missile would have had to hit the president on the right side or the front of the head. It would have been miraculous if he had survived that type of wound."

'It seems that a photograph taken at Bethesda Hospital during the autopsy performed there shows a different head wound than the one you describe. Can you explain that, Doctor?"

"I saw that photograph, Mr. Burke," McClelland admitted. "Actually, for this photograph, someone pulled a flap of scalp over Kennedy's fatal wound, changing the appearance of the wound. There was a massive hole in the back of his head, Mr. Burke, which, in my opinion, was an exit wound. I looked at that hole from about 18 inches away for about 12 minutes. I know what I saw."

Ryan gave Dr. McClellan a sheet of paper on which the diagram of the back of a man's head had been drawn.

"Would you please draw on this figure the wound you saw on the president's head?"

"You'll have to bear with me, Mr. Ryan. I'm not much of an artist. But, we doctors are expected to include drawings, however crude, with our reports of wounds we treat in the ER. So, I'll do my best."

The doctor drew a square-shaped wound on the rear right of the head.

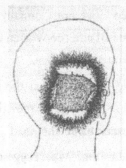

"This will do very nicely, Doctor. Do you have anything else to add?"

"Not right now," Mr. Ryan, "But if I think of anything, my secretary has your number.

"Yes, of course, Doctor. Thank you for coming."

***

That evening, Ryan and Burke were eating in the Howard Johnson restaurant.

"Do you have any off-the-cuff impressions, Harold?" Burke asked his partner.

"Anger," he responded. "The people I interviewed were angry and confused."

"What about?"

"They were angry that the folks in Washington were so determined to blame Oswald for everything despite a good deal of evidence to the contrary."

"And the confusion," Burke asked. "What's that all about?"

"Why? They ask, "Why has everyone in Washington been avoiding and denying the evidence and testimony that suggests there was more than one shooter?"

"What about the people you interviewed, Mike?"

"Pretty much the same, Harold," Burke said. "The folks I interviewed were also puzzled, and for the same reasons. They definitely do not believe that anyone in Washington sought the truth. In fact, the retired Dallas Chief of Police believes that LBJ and his buddy, Hoover, decided on the one-shooter scenario before the body of Kennedy had even arrived in Washington. Once that decision had been made, he thinks they put pressure on everyone else to ignore evidence that didn't support that conclusion. Even Governor Connally and his wife don't believe the single shooter decisions of the FBI and the Warren Commission. They believe that Kennedy was hit from the front at least once."

Ryan added, "That would jibe with what the Parkland people told me, too. Depending upon whom you're listening to, they think at least one and probably two bullets hit Kennedy from the front."

"Before we go back to the room," Mike suggested, "let's take a drive down to Dealey Plaza and walk the ground. Seems ta' me that we ought to at least do that before we interview any more of the witnesses. What do ya' think?"

"Makes sense. Let me get my stuff."

***

Not knowing much about downtown Dallas, the two men wandered drove around some before finding their way to the plaza. They still had plenty of light, though, when they arrived at their destination.

They turned off Houston west onto Elm Street, just as the president's motorcade had done back on November 22nd, 1963.

"Wow!" Burke exclaimed. "I really had to slow down to make that turn. No wonder Police Commissioner Curry said it was an ideal route for an assassination."

"Right," Ryan agreed. "Sitting in the back seat of an open vehicle, a person would have been an easy target from any of the tall buildings around here."

"Don't forget the knoll to our right or the overpass ahead, too, Harold."

"Exactly."

"Why don't you park on the street?" Ryan asked. "I'd like to walk up there and stand behind that wooden fence I've heard so much about."

"So would I," Burke agreed.

When they reached the top of the knoll, they walked around the back of the fence and looked down the slope toward Elm Street.

"This is a great spot for a shooter," Ryan said. "With so many people around to watch the parade, it took nerve to shoot from here."

"From the testimony taken to the Commission, it appears to me that the role of the fake Secret Service guys up here was to keep potential witnesses away."

"Seems like that part of the plot worked."

"Not really, Harold," Mike said. "We've got plenty of witnesses. But their testimony didn't support the single shooter conclusion the commission and FBI had settled on. So their statements were buried in the reports and not followed up with any investigation at all. Tomorrow, I'm going to talk with a guy who was standing on that tower back there. Right now, I'm going to climb up there and have a look before it gets dark. You want to go with me or wait here?"

"I'm not as spry as you, Mike," Harold chuckled. "You go ahead. I'll meet you back at the car."

By the time Harold stood back at their car, Mike had reached the tower and had begun to climb to its top platform.

Suddenly, the passenger window alongside Harold shattered. He dropped to the ground as he heard the report from a gun of some kind that followed.

Meanwhile, Mike stood atop the tower. He grabbed his left arm and dropped prone as the report of another gunshot echoed in the evening air.

Then everything was quiet.

Mike crept carefully down the tower's staircase to the ground. Harold stayed where he was on the ground by the car and waited.

By the time Mike reached the car, Harold had thought it safe enough to get into the vehicle. Mike joined him, and they headed back to their motel.

"What the hell!" Harold exclaimed. "I think I heard a second shot. Are you all right, Mike?"

"Barely," he answered. "I got a crease on my left arm. Seems like there were two shooters, don't you think?"

"Probably. We must be doing something right for someone to try to frighten us off."

"Ya' think?" Mike responded. "Now what do you want to do, partner?"

"For starters, I think we head for Parkland Hospital and have the ER people look at that arm."

"It hardly seems worth the trouble. It's just a scratch, Harold."

"That might be true. But by going there, we've established a record of the incident. We may find it important that we did that."

"You're the lawyer here," Mike admitted. "So it's to Parkland we go."

After they arrived at the ER room, the insurance and other paperwork took over an hour to complete before any medical personnel were allowed to look at the wound.

Then, a quick look by the doctor on duty, a tetanus shot, and a few minutes to clean and bandage the wound by one of the nurses had Mike out the door a few minutes later.

Back at Howard Johnson's, they went to the restaurant for coffee and conversation. Mike ordered a piece of cherry pie, too.

"How's the arm, Mike?"

"It's beginning to smart and stiffen up some."

"Take some more aspirin. It's a wonder drug. Cures most everything, don't you know."

"We'll see." Mike swallowed two tablets.

"You know," Mike told Harold. "I still have my FBI permit to carry a concealed weapon. I think I'll go out tomorrow and buy me a handgun. We were helpless out there tonight."

"Do you really think that a handgun would have done much for us against a couple of rifles with scopes?"

"Probably not, Harold. But it will make me feel better."

"There's something to be said for that. You're not going to tell your wife about this, are you?"

"I surely will not tell her on the phone. But unless I keep a shirt on, even in bed, I don't know how I can keep from telling her about this groove on my arm."

"You have a point. Going to tell your buddy Sullivan at the Bureau about it?"

"I don't know if that it'll do much good. But if I complain to my boss Conyers, he might raise hell with Hoover; get him to call off the dogs."

"That might work. Hoover did promise Conyers his cooperation, didn't he?"

"Yes, he did. So I think I'll try that tack first."

"What have you got tomorrow, Mike?"

"Well, if I'm sufficiently recovered from my battle wounds, I have interviews with several witnesses. I also plan to talk with the pair who saw Oswald in the lunch room on the second floor seconds after the president was shot."

"Are you going to talk with the Dallas mayor whose brother was fired by JFK right after the Bay of Pigs fiasco? "

"If he shows up, he's on the list for Friday. "

"How about you, Harold?"

"I have more medical people lined up. Dr. Perry has been ducking me, so I'll be trying to nail him down today. "He's the one who was pressured to change his testimony and say that the throat wound might have been an exit wound. The information I have is that during the evening of November 22nd, he began receiving harassing phone calls, asking him to change what he had said earlier that day about the throat wound. Both he and Dr. Clark had told reporters at a press conference held on the afternoon of November 22nd that the throat wound was one of entry and identified it that way in their written report of the treatment given President Kennedy in the trauma room. So he is understandably wary of anyone from Washington, and in particular, anyone asking questions about his ER actions and the later press conference of November 22nd,1963."

"Think you'll get the truth out of him?"

"I doubt it. And I can't blame him. He's got a career to think of. Besides, with both the FBI report and the Warren Commission report as the government's official position, any debate is over. Why would he expose himself any further for no purpose? So, to answer your question, I don't think we'll get anything out of him. But I'd like to hear him say it anyway."

"We may not have to, Harold," Burke interjected.

"Because?"

"Because the Zapruder film clearly shows President Kennedy's reaction to being hit in the throat while facing the overpass, that is, while he was looking to the right front. This is quite clear on the original still photographs the *Life Magazine* people printed in their edition of November 29, 1963," Burke reminded his colleague. "In a caption with their photograph, the *Life Magazine* people also stated that his car was 75 yards beyond the Book Depository Building when he was hit in the throat."

"Hard to understand how the FBI and the Warren Commission managed to disregard such clear evidence."

"Isn't that why we're here, Harold?"

"Right."

"Let's hit the sack," Mike suggested. "I need some sleep."

"Come on, my wounded warrior partner. I'll tuck you in myself."

"Spare me, please."

"I'm just trying to help out, ol' buddy."

***

The next morning, Mike was in the FBI conference room to conduct his first interview of the day.

"Good morning Mr. Weitzman," Mike began. "Thank you for coming."

"It's quite all right, Mr. Burke. I'll do anything I can to help with any confusion you might have with the statement I made about finding that rifle in the Book Depository Building."

"I've read the statement you gave on November 23 to a notary public. Maybe you could expand on it some."

"Captain Fritz of the Dallas Police Department and Deputy Sheriff Craig arrived at that building right after me, as did Deputy Sheriff Boone. Fritz ordered all of the sixth floor sealed off and searched. Then, all of us began searching the sixth floor of the building. Sheriff's Deputies Boone and Craig looked behind some boxes staked at the head of the stairwell in the northeast corner of the sixth floor. They spotted a weapon. They called Fritz and Captain Day of the Dallas police over. First, they took some pictures, then Fritz held it up by its strap and asked if anyone knew what kind of weapon it was. I came over, looked at it, and identified it as a 7.65 Mauser. As a matter of fact, stamped right on the barrel of the rifle, clear as day, was 7.65 Mauser."

"You're sure, Mr. Weitzman?"

"As I swore in my affidavit, the weapon we found was a 7.65 Mauser bolt action rifle. It had a 4/18 scope on it as well. As I said in my statement, it was about 1:20 PM when it was found. Captain Fritz took the weapon, and I went back to the sheriff's office."

"Are you sure it was not a Mannlicher-Carcano, Italian-made rifle that was found?"

Weitzman signed in exasperation. "No sir," he repeated. "Stamped right on the barrel of the weapon that was found on the afternoon of November 22nd and the one Captain Fritz took, was 7.65 Mauser. I sold guns in a sportsman's shop for a number of years, Mr. Burke. So I know what I saw. The rifle we found was not an Italian-made Mannlicher-Cearcano rifle. It was a 7.65 Mauser."

"Did you or the others find anything else out of the ordinary on the sixth floor when you were searching, like another weapon?"

"No, sir. After we found the rifle, Captain Fritz sort of dismissed us."

"Anything you want to add to the statement you made on November 23rd, 1963?"

"Just seems odd to me, Mr. Burke, that there's a mix-up about which rifle was used for the shots fired from the sixth-floor window of the Book Depository Building. In all my years in law enforcement, bullets taken from the body of the victim were used to help identify the weapon used in the shooting. In this case, the Mauser rifle Boone and Craig found on the sixth floor seems to have been ignored by the FBI. Instead, an Italian-made weapon was identified as the weapon used to kill President Kennedy. How did that happen?"

"I don't know exactly, Mr. Weitzman," Burke told him.

Burke went on, "But a bullet was found lying on one of the gurneys in the Parkland ER. It is said to have come from the Italian-made rifle, not a Mauser. And three shell casings found by a window on the sixth floor of the Book Depository were said to have come from an Italian-made rifle, too."

Burke then asked, "But you searched the sixth floor. Where do you think the Italian rifle came from?"

"Beats me, Mr. Burke," Weitzman declared. "I know the only rifle we found on the sixth floor of that building on the afternoon of the assassination was a 7.65 Mauser."

"Quite a mystery, it would appear," Burke stated.

Weitzman continued. "It would seem so. But wouldn't a bullet taken from the president at his autopsy or from Governor Connally when they operated on him answer that question?"

"I suppose," Burke agreed. "Evidently, neither was done."

"Around here, that's sort a' routine in a murder case where firearms are involved. I gotta believe that if an official autopsy was done at Parkland as Texas law requires, we wouldn't have to ask these questions."

"You would think so, Mr. Weitzman."

"Just seems like a strange way to proceed with such an important investigation," Weitzman concluded.

"A lot of Americans wonder about that, too, Mr. Weitzman. That's why I'm here; to take another look at some of these things. Do you have anything else?"

"As a matter of fact, I do," Weitzman responded. "Before I went to the Book Depository to help search for the weapon, I had run up onto the Grassy Knoll by the picket fence. I was stopped there by a man who showed me a Secret Service ID and told me and some others to get out of the area. Later, I identified that man from a bunch of photographs as Bernard Barker, who, I was told, had some kind of connection with the CIA."

"Were you ever questioned officially about this?" Burke asked.

"No, sir. I was never asked about him again. But other people encountered him that day, too, just like me. I saw that happen. I've got something else to show you, Mr. Burke," Weitzman added. "Would you take a look at these two photographs?"

Weitzman placed one of the prints on the table in front of Burke.

"I clipped this one from our Dallas newspaper. Do you recognize the weapon being held up by Lieutenant Day at a local press conference?"

"This appears to be a photograph of a Mannlicher-Carcano rifle," Burke said.

"Correct," Weitzman said. "Now, look at this one held by Oswald."

"I got this photograph from the Warren Commission Report. Do you see any difference in the two rifles?"

No, I don't."

"If you look at the rifle held by the person identified as Oswald, you will note that the rifle sling swivels are mounted on the bottom of the stock."

Burke picked up the photo and took a close look at it. "I can see that, yes."

"Now, Mr. Burke," Weitzman continued, "look at the photo of the Mannli-cher-Carcano rifle the Commission claims is the rifle used to kill the president and wound the governor. It's the rifle held by Captain Day of the Dallas Police Department at a press conference announcing the discovery of the murder weapon."

Burke picked up that photo and looked closely. "What am I looking for?"

"You might notice that the swivels holding the sling on that rifle Day is holding are mounted on the left side of the stock."

"Oh, my goodness," Burke exclaimed. "They're not the same weapon, Mr. Weitzman!"

"My thought exactly, sir."

"This business of the weapon gets stranger and stranger."

Weitzman got up, shook Burke's hand, and prepared to leave.

"Any way I can help, you just let me know, Mr. Burke."

"Thank you, I will."

***

Mr. Sam Holland was the next person waiting in the hallway.

After the preliminary questions had been answered, Burke asked. "Exactly where were you standing when you heard the first shot, Mr. Holland?"

"I was standing atop the triple underpass. I had a direct look at the approaching vehicles when I heard the first shot. Then I heard three other shots. One of them seemed to hit President Kennedy in the face, and his head jerked back."

"Did you see where the shots came from?"

"Yes. I saw a puff of smoke coming up from under the trees back of the wooden fence at the top of the Grassy Knoll. That was the third or fourth shot fired, the one that hit President Kennedy in the face."

"Anyone else see what you saw?"

"Yes. A member of the Dallas Police Department was standing right there with me and several other railroad workers, too. After the shots, the policeman ran toward the Book Depository Building."

"You gave this information to the FBI?"

"I did," Holland said. "The Sunday following the assassination, they were at my house. I told them four shots. But, they didn't take what I told them seriously."

"How did you know that?"

Holland replied. "I feel that way because they kept saying three or four shots. I corrected them, but they weren't listening, I guess. I know what I heard. The other guys watching with me saw and heard the same thing. Ya know, Mr. Burke," Holland concluded. "I don't think those big shots were really serious about investigating the assassination."

"What do you think they were trying to do, then?"

"I believe they had decided early on that one shooter fired three shots and killed the president and wounded our governor. Once they had reached that conclusion, they weren't interested in any evidence which challenged that."

"I think you're right on track, Mr. Holland."

***

Before Burke could begin his next interview, he was handed a note from one of the secretaries.

He was to call home immediately.

I hope nothing's wrong with one of the kids.

Mike's wife answered the phone after the first ring.

"Hi there," he said cheerfully. "What's up?"

"Michael. You've got to come right home."

"Are the kids all right?" he responded. "What's wrong?"

"I got a threatening call last night around midnight."

"Oh, shit!" Mike almost shouted. "What did the guy say?"

"He said for you to stop this investigation, or something might happen to the kids on their way to school. He knew their names and even the name of the street they use when they walk to school. I told him to go to hell and hung up."

"Good for you, sweetheart," Mike told her. "Are you all right now?"

"I was," Marilyn told him. "Until this morning when I went out to go to the store, I found two tires flat on the car. The service guy said holes had been punched into them with something like an ice pick."

"Oh, crap!" Mike repeated.

"You've got to do something."

"I will, sweetheart," Mike assured her. "First, I'm going to be on the first flight back. Then I'm going to talk to Conyers. He has to put a stop to this, or I'm outta here. I'll call you later with my flight information as soon as I have it."

"We need you home, Michael."

"Don't worry, Marilyn. I'll be home as fast as I can. Any strange calls, just hang up. Don't even listen to 'em."

***

Burke put in a call to the Parkland Hospital for Harold Ryan. Then, he called the airline for flight information. He couldn't get back to Washington until the next morning. So he booked his flight for that time.

It wasn't long before he was called to a phone; it was Ryan.

"You called?" Harold began.

Burke explained the situation and the flight arrangement for his return to Washington.

"Hell, Mike," Ryan told him. "I can take the interviews you've scheduled for tomorrow. I've pretty well squeezed the Parkland well dry. How is your family taking all this?"

"Surprisingly well, I think. Marilyn seems pretty calm. But she wants me home right now."

"Understandable."

"Did you get to Perry, Harold?"

"No, I didn't. But we have the transcript of what he said repeatedly during his press conference on November 22 about the throat wound being an entry wound before the feds put pressure on him to alter his testimony. And I doubt if he's going to stick his neck out now. We've got plenty without him, anyway. You can bring me up to speed about your interviews at dinner tonight, Mike. I'll take you to the airport in the morning and follow you to D.C. when I've finished here in Dallas."

"That'll work. I'll pick you up at 4 o'clock today."

"See you then."

***

Later, as Burke was getting ready to leave to meet Ryan, there was a knock on the door.

He opened it to see two young ladies standing in the hall.

"Mr. Burke?"

"Yes, I'm Michael Burke," he answered. "How can I help you?"

"I'm Mary Woodward, and this is Maggie Brown. We both work at the *Dallas Morning News*. We heard that you were going to interview witnesses to the Kennedy assassination today, so we got ahold of your wife at your home in Maryland. She told us to just show up here. I hope you don't mind our chasing you down like that, but we have information about the assassination that might interest you?"

"I don't mind at all. How does the assassination involve you ladies?"

"We have some information the Warren Commission people refused to take from us. Would you like to hear what we heard and saw that day?"

"Yes, I would," Burke said. "Please come in and take a seat."

Once they were seated, Burke took down the basic personal information from each of them just like he did before he began all of his interviews.

Then he asked. "Please show me on this map where you were standing that day and what you heard."

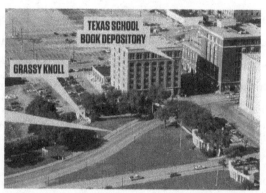

"Four of us were standing on the grass looking toward Elm Street as the motorcade rounded the turn from Huston and came toward us. We were a few yards down from the wooden fence." Ms. Woodward related.

Maggie Brown said, "Suddenly, we heard a loud ear-shattering noise behind us, almost like a clap of thunder. We all fell to the ground."

"Our story was in the *Morning News* the next day, but none of us were called by the Warren Commission people to tell what we heard on the Grassy Knoll."

"Do you have anything else to add, ladies?" Mike asked.

The two women looked at one another and then looked at Burke.

Maggie Brown said, "No, that's it, Mr. Burke."

"Is what we told you of any help in your investigation?" Mary Woodward asked.

"Yes, it is," Burke told them. "And I appreciate you taking the time to tell me. Thank you."

"There was a young man waiting for you out in the hall. I think he wants to talk with you, too." Maggie told Burke.

Sure enough, there was.

***

"Are you waiting to see me?"

"Yes, I am, Mr. Burke. My name is Gordon Arnold. Do you have a few minutes for me?"

"Sure do. Please come in and have a seat."

First, Burke asked for and received the usual background information. Then, he began.

"So, Mr. Arnold, you were present in Dallas on November 22nd, 1963?"

"Yes, sir, I was," he responded. "Actually, I was walking on the Grassy Knoll in back of the picket fence when I was stopped by a guy in a light-colored suit who told me that I should not the there. When I challenged that order, he showed me a badge and said he was Secret Service. I had just finished army basic training and was used to taking orders and obeying them. So I did what he told me, walked around the front of the fence, and found an elevated spot under the trees where I could film the motorcade as it turned onto Elm Street from Houston. Just after the president's car rounded the corner onto Elm, a shot went off over my left shoulder. I felt the bullet rather than heard it, and it went right by my left ear. I had just gotten out of basic training and knew that live ammunition had just been fired. It was being fired over my head. I hit the dirt," Arnold continued. "Then I heard two shots. Before I knew it, someone was kicking my butt and telling me to get up. It was a policeman. Another policeman came up with a gun drawn. One of them demanded that I give him my camera. After I did, he tore out the film and tossed my camera back to me."

"What did you do then, Mr. Arnold?"

"I just wanted to get away from that guy with the gun. So I went back to my car and drove out of the parking lot unchallenged. Two days later, I reported for duty at Fort Wainright in Alaska. I recently returned to this area and read in the papers that you were looking for information about the assassination. So, I called the paper, and they told me where to find you."

"Have you told your story to anyone else since the assassination?"

"Only my family knows about my experience, Mr. Burke," Arnold said. "Remember, I was just an army grunt. I didn't need to paint a target on my chest by coming forward. Who knew what might have happened if I had?" Maybe I'd find myself shipped to Vietnam for my trouble. Besides, after the Warren Commission decided that all the shots came from behind the president, I figured I had just misheard those shots on the Grassy Knoll."

"Just so you know, Mr. Arnold," Burke told him. "You aren't alone in what you experienced that day. A number of others have identified shots coming from that same area."

"So, I'm not crazy after all," Arnold sighed. "That's a relief. But, if there are others, why did the Warren Commission and the FBI insist that all the shots came from the Book Depository building behind the president?"

"To answer that question is why I'm here in Dallas talking with people like you. With your help, maybe we'll discover the truth after all."

"I hope so, Mr. Burke."

***

Later, over dinner, the two men shared some observations from their day.

"My talk with Seymour Weitzman reminded me of something," Mike said.

"Refresh my memory about Weitzman," Harold asked.

Burke brought him up to date on Seymour Weitzman; then, he continued.

"Exhibit #399 is the pristine bullet found on the gurney at Parkland. Supposedly it is the bullet that was fired from Oswald's Italian-made rifle and went through the back of Kennedy's neck and into Connally."

"Isn't that the one Lane called the 'Magic Bullet'?"

"The very one," Burke agreed. "I looked in my copy of the Commission's final report and read about the tests they authorized. They had ballistics people fire bullets into animal carcasses. All the bullets fired by the Commission's ballistics experts in those tests became flattened or distorted. Nevertheless, the Commission ignored these experts. Instead, they insisted that the undamaged bullet found on a gurney at Parkland Hospital was the one which caused the throat wound in Kennedy and all the wounds in Connally, seven in all."

"No wonder Lane, in his book, '*Rush to Judgment*,' called that single bullet the 'Magic Bullet,'" Ryan said.

FBI OFFICE IN WASHINGTON

"Mrs. Gandy," Hoover said over his intercom to his secretary. "Please tell Mr. Sullivan I'd like to see him immediately."

"Yes, sir."

It couldn't have been more than five minutes before Hoover's phone rang. "Yes, Helen?"

"Mr. Sullivan is here, sir."

"Have him come in."

The door opened, and Sullivan entered.

"Yes, sir?" He approached Hoover's desk and was not asked to sit. Instead, he was left standing like a schoolboy who had misbehaved.

"What in hell is this about Burke's family being harassed?"

"Nothing serious, sir," Sullivan answered. "Just some mild pressure, I assure you."

"Your mild pressure has enraged the chairman of an important Congressional committee. I received a call from John Conyers not ten minutes ago. He heard of the late-night call to Burke's home and the damage done to the tires of the Burke vehicle. He assumed we were behind it and is one very angry congressman. Congressman Ford's call followed his by seconds. Need I tell you that we do not need this?"

"No, sir."

'If that isn't bad enough, former Congressman Ryan was fired upon in Dallas last evening as he walked around Dealey Plaza. Thankfully, the shot missed him and only damaged one of our own vehicles. Not only that, but Michael Burke, you remember him; your man Burke was treated at Parkland Hospital Emergency last night for a gunshot wound to his arm. You have very possibly made this nothing investigation into something of an issue. The entire exercise was only authorized to satisfy some public pressure by taking another look at our investigation of the Kennedy assassination. It was only intended to recycle and endorse our report and that of the Warren Commission; end of story. My Lord, man! Conyers and Ford only assigned a low-level staffer and a washed-up former Congressman to the job. They didn't even give them clerical support. Didn't that tell you something, Sullivan?"

Hoover didn't wait for a response. He was in a rage.

"Now we have the Chairman of the House Committee on the Judiciary and the committee's Minority Leader, Congressman Ford, wondering what we have to hide that justified the harassment of their staffer's family, presumably by FBI agents, and the committee's investigators being fired upon by unknown assailants, probably other FBI agents. Thanks to you, we have these important men who have always been our allies on the Hill, really angry with us. I thought you had this under control, Sullivan."

"It is, sir, I assure you."

"You had better regain control, Mr. Sullivan. Or you will find yourself in Omaha, Nebraska, or on border patrol duty behind a dog sled in Alaska. Do I make myself clear?"

"Yes, sir."

Not knowing if the chewing-out was over, Sullivan stood there for a moment longer.

"Don't you have some damage control work to do?"

"Yes, sir."

"Then get out of here and do it right this time."

SILVER SPRING

Burke pulled into his Silver Spring driveway. He had called his wife as soon as his plane had gotten him to Baltimore earlier that afternoon. A rental car accomplished the rest.

He dropped his bag on the floor of the back room and searched for her.

In the front room, Marilyn left the couch and rushed into his arms. They stood still, just holding one another.

"How are you, sweetheart?"

"There were more calls last night, Michael," she reported. "I didn't know if it might be you, so I answered each time it rang. But as soon as I heard a strange voice, I hung up. I didn't sleep a wink."

"I'm so sorry."

"This morning, when the girls opened the front door to leave for school, they discovered a dead cat on the porch."

"God damn it!"

"I got them inside and drove them to school," Marilyn continued. "When I used our garden shovel to pick up the dead animal, I noticed it had been strangled."

"Damn it to hell!" Mike hissed. "I'll get those bastards."

Marilyn leaned back and looked into his eyes.

"I want you to get them. I don't want you to quit, Michael," she said fiercely. "I want you to destroy them. Keep at it until you can show them up for the lying scum they are. Will you do that for me, Michael?"

"I'll do that for us, sweetheart. Believe me, I will."

His wife was shaking when he pulled her back into his embrace. He could feel her sob.

Those sons-a'-bitches. I'll teach them a lesson they'll not soon forget.

"I need you to hold me, Michael," Marilyn said through her tears. "Just hold me."

Michael squeezed his wife closer as they stood in the living room.

***

Burke and his wife drove to the daycare school and picked up their youngest, Jackie. Then they went to the elementary school and waited for Susan and Ann to be dismissed for the day.

"Daddy! Daddy!" The girls shouted as they jumped into the back seat of the car. "We missed you." The two oldest girls leaned over the back seat and gave him hugs.

"I missed you too, guys," he said. "Who wants to go with me to McDonald's for an after-school treat?"

"We do!" Susan and Ann shouted.

"Hooray," Jackie shouted. "I want a chocolate sundae."

"How about you, ladies?" Mike asked the others. "What do you want?"

"I want chicken nuggets and fries," Ann announced.

"Me, too," Susan said.

"Good choice."

Then Mike asked their mother. "What do you want, Mom?"

"I think I'll have a cheeseburger, small fries, and a cola."

"How about you, Dad?" she asked. "Are you a hungry dude today?"

"You bet I am," he responded. "I missed lunch. So I think I'll have a big double cheeseburger, fries, and a chocolate shake."

Susan leaned over the front seat and whispered to her mother.

"Mom," Susan asked. "Did you tell Dad about the cat?"

"Yes, I did," she whispered back. "But I think we'll talk about that when we get home. Is that OK with you?"

Of course, both ends of the exchange were loud enough for all to hear.

"Good idea, Mom," Ann said. "Let's go to McDonald's, Dad."

"Hooray!" Jackie agreed.

***

Everyone was still full from their treat when suppertime rolled around in the Burke household. So everyone had a small bowl of cereal.

Once they had washed up and put on their jammies, the children all sat on their beds. Instead of just their dad, Marilyn joined them.

Mike began the conversation. "Who wants to tell me what she saw on our porch this morning?"

Ann was the first to speak up.

"Someone left a dead kitten on the porch, Dad."

"It was really gross," Susan added.

"What did you see, Jackie?" Marilyn asked.

"You pulled me back into the house before I could, Mom," Jackie answered. "Don't you remember that?"

"Oh ya'," Marilyn agreed. "I forgot."

"Why would someone do that, Dad?" Susan asked.

"Remember last Halloween when we went through all the treats our neighbors gave you?"

"Oh, ya'," Ann answered. "You were worried someone might have put something in the candy to hurt us."

"Ya'," Susan added. "You wouldn't even let us keep the apples we were given."

"And you cut up all the candy bars in our bags, too." Ann reminded everyone.

"Mom and I did that because the police announced that some bad person had given poisoned fruit to trick-or-treaters the previous Halloween."

"But why did you cut up the candy bars we got, Dad?"

"Because the year before, some bad person put needles into the candy they gave out."

"Why would anyone want to hurt children?" Susan asked.

Marilyn said, "It is strange, isn't it?" Marilyn said. "I expect that kind of person is just hateful and wants to hurt people."

"They ought to be arrested and put in jail," Ann decided.

"So, kids," Mike began, "if Mom and I had found anything bad in the candy, we would have told the police. They would then have visited the houses where you got your candy and questioned people."

"That way, they could find the bad people, for sure," Marilyn told them.

"As for the dead kitten," Mike began. "There is probably someone in our area who thought it would be funny to scare us. They probably don't even know us. But I want you guys to stay around the yard for a while, OK?"

"Can't we even walk down to Mary's house?" Ann asked.

"Or even go across the street to play with the Miles boys?" Susan added.

"Not for a while, girls," Marilyn told them. "But I'll sit on the front porch after you come home from school. That way, after you change your clothes and have your snack, you can play out in front with your friends. I'll keep a lookout, so you won't have to worry about the bad people who put the cat on our porch."

"Remember, Mom," Susan said. "We have Mr. Joe next door, too."

"Good point, Susan," Mike agreed. "I'll have a talk with him. I'm sure he'll help us keep a lookout, too."

"What will you be looking for, anyway?" Ann asked.

"Good question, Ann," Mike told her. "Mom and I are not sure exactly. But if a stranger comes into our block, Mom or Mr. Joe will know it. You just need to remember not to even *talk* to a stranger. Just walk away from that person. And never, ever should you get into a stranger's car. If someone puts a hand on you, start screaming at the top of your lungs and run for home," Mike concluded.

"Do you understand what Dad is telling you, girls?" their mother asked.

Jackie had already fallen asleep. But her sisters answered. "Yes, Mother."

"Don't just, 'yes, Mother' me, you two," Marilyn snapped. "This is important. Do you understand what Dad just told you?

"Susan?"

"Yes, Mother, I understand."

"Ann?"

"Yes, Mother, I understand."

Marilyn left Mike in the bedroom.

"By the way, girls," Mike added. "Your little sister doesn't understand this stuff. You have to look after her. OK?"

"Yes, Dad, we will," Susan replied. Then she socked her pillow a couple of times and snuggled under her blankets. "Goodnight, Dad. I'm glad you're home."

Ann slid under her blankets and moved close to her sister. "I hope you stay home for a while, Dad," she added. "I love you."

"Love you, too, girls," he said as he left their room.

Mike and Marilyn sat on the couch in the living room with their coffee. Mike told her all about his trip to Dallas. She told him again about the phone calls, the flat tires, and the cat episode.

"I think we need to keep a log of these calls," he told her. "Conyers assures me that he had gotten such stuff stopped. But just the same, let's be prepared."

He got a pad of paper and a pencil. Marilyn then told him the gist of each call she had taken the last two days. He even listed the hang-ups.

Of course, he also wrote down all the details of the flat tires and the dead cat incident.

"I'm going to share all this stuff with Conyers and Ford. I called them from the Dallas airport yesterday while I was waiting for my flight. They told me that they had called Hoover directly and read the riot act to him. He assured them that he knew nothing of this business."

Marilyn interrupted, "Of course, he wouldn't get his hands dirty. He'd have someone else do it. You think he had your old boss Sullivan handle it?"

"Probably, sweetheart," Mike said. "But Hoover assured both of them that his office would continue to support our investigation."

Marilyn had finished her coffee, and she snuggled up to her husband.

"So, my knight in shining armor, what's next?"

Mike put his arm around his wife and kissed her.

"I've missed you so," he told her. "I'm sorry they involved you in this business."

"It's not your fault, Michael," she assured him. "Actually, I'm sort of glad it happened."

That comment got Mike's attention.

"Wow!" he said, sitting up straight. "Where did that come from?"

"I guess it came from my need to be more fully involved in your life. Don't you see, Michael? They've dragged me into this investigation. Now, I want you to thoroughly investigate their cover-up and reveal it to the public. I want them embarrassed and their power destroyed. And I want to help you do it."

"Does that mean you're willing to endure more of the harassment you have just encountered?"

"If that's what's needed to bring them down, yes."

"So you're actually willing to join me in this investigation?"

"What is your first assignment, Sir Knight?"

Michael smiled and pulled his wife back into his arms.

"First, fair maiden, you can give me a big hug and a long, very wet kiss."

"Your wish is my command. But only on one condition."

"And what would that condition be?"

"That this time, we make it to that soft bed in the guest bedroom."

"You drive a hard bargain, woman."

OFFICES OF THE HOUSE COMMITTEE ON THE JUDICIARY

"Yes, Mike," John Conyers told Burke. "You heard me correctly; I want you and Ryan to continue this investigation."

"Play around the edges, or do a thorough job, sir?"

"I will admit that initially, this probe was more for public relations than substance. But now the Bureau has changed that with their treatment of your family and their attack on you and Ryan. They must be afraid of something. I'd like you to find out what's behind that fear; get to the heart of the matter. If they played loose with the facts back in '63, I want you to detail it as completely as possible. The public already thinks the FBI report of December 1963 was a cover-up. If it was, so be it. Put it under a microscope, Mike. Shake out the facts. Lay it all out there. The Bureau opened the door; let's walk through it. And let the chips fall where they may."

Mike agreed. "That's fine, sir. But if Ryan and I are chained to a desk digging through documents, we'll not get out into the field. Can you give us some researchers and clerical people?"

"You can have two researchers and one clerical person," Conyers told him. "You have anyone in mind?"

"My wife wants to help. She is so mad at those guys she can hardly contain herself. She has a degree in English, so I'd like her to do our scheduling and some research from our home in Maryland. As for the others, you pick 'em, sir."

"Get it done, Mike. Bring your wife in tomorrow to get all her paperwork done. I'll have the rest of the staff on board the first of the week. You can vet them then, OK?"

"Yes, sir."

"How's the wound on your arm?"

"Healing nicely, sir," Mike told him. "Every time it hurts, I'm motivated to work harder."

"Atta' boy. Now, get outta here and back to work."

"Yes, sir."

***

Harold Ryan was back in the Washington office the first of the week. Burke brought him up to date on developments.

"My goodness, Burke," he exclaimed. "You certainly have been a busy guy since I last saw you."

"Evidently, Conyers and Ford hit the wall when they heard what happened at my home and to us in Dallas. They want us to do a serious job on this thing."

"Glory be," Ryan said. "Makes one almost believe in miracles, doesn't it?"

"Yup. In guardian angels, too," Mike replied.

"Well, my friend, let's not look at a gift horse in the mouth. Let's get on with it. We need a plan. Do you have one?"

"I have the list of interviews I had planned to conduct when I returned from Dallas. I've got a couple to add to that list. How about you?"

"High on my list is Kennedy's doctor, Admiral Burkley. The doctors who did the autopsy at Bethesda Hospital and the others who were in attendance are next. When are you going to see the rifle experts who participated in the reenactments?"

"They're on my list, and so is Arlen Specter. How about Boggs, Russell, and Cooper? You still want to do those interviews?"

"Yes, I do. Being a former Congressman, and the 'good ole boy club' being what it is, I think it will work best if I see those commission members," Ryan told him.

"Marilyn has already started making my appointments. Give her a call with your list, and she'll get on that, too."

Thanks, I'll do that when we're done here. But I think I'll call Boggs and the two Senators myself."

***

It took a few days to get the staff organized and focused on their tasks, but by the end of the week, they were digging through both the FBI report and the Warren Commission report.

Their first task was to identify everyone who had testified, been interviewed, or given affidavits during the two investigations conducted after the assassination.

The staff noted the address, working history, and testimony of each person. The researchers also recorded where each person was at the time of the shooting and whom they first told about what they saw.

All of this was cross-referenced.

Marilyn, too, was off and running. By the end of the week, she had arranged several appointments for both Mike and Ryan.

***

Ryan's first meeting was with his old colleague, Congressman Hale Boggs.

Harold was shown into the Congressman's office.

"Well, I'll be damned," Boggs came out of his chair, hand extended. "How tha' hell are you, Harold?"

"I'm getting by," he replied. "And you?"

"Middlin' well for a country boy, Harold," Boggs joked. "I hear you almost got your tail shot off in Dallas last week."

"Still no secrets in Washington, I see," Harold laughed.

"Never were, never will be," Boggs said.

"Maybe they missed on purpose," Harold surmised. "Cus' if someone really wanted to hit me with a bullet, they probably could've."

"I suppose," Boggs agreed. "How can I help you, ol' friend?"

"You can tell me why you caved on that 'single bullet' business when you served on the Warren Commission."

"That was supposed to be a secret, ya' know."

Both men laughed. "No secrets in this town, remember," Harold joked.

"Am I speaking for some record, or is this just between two old comrades?"

"Just between you, me, and the lamppost, ol' buddy."

"No tape recorders or hidden microphones?"

"Nary a one."

"All right." Boggs began in a whisper. "Where do I start?

"On the very day the president was murdered, the folks over at the FBI decided that the killing had to have been the work of one shooter. For it to be otherwise, an entirely different and more lengthy investigation would have been necessary. If that had happened, then 'Katie bar the door.' And Hoover and LBJ were terrified of that."

"What were they so afraid of, Hale?"

"Who knew where the evidence might take the country? There were press reports that Cuba and the Russians had played a part in the assassination. Revelations might have forced us to blame Castro and possibly bring on a war with the Soviet Union. That was the big fear that drove LBJ. Hoover and Earl Warren, too. So it was decided by the FBI that a sad-sack misfit, Oswald, would be the sole shooter. Then everything else sorta fell into place, sorta like dominoes."

"I can see that," Ryan agreed.

"Exactly. Now, follow me on this, Harold," Boggs continued. "First, the single shooter scenario meant that the throat wound could not be one of entry. It had to be an exit wound. Second, all the shots had to have come from behind. The FBI Report released in early December 1963 laid all that out. They insisted that three shots caused three wounds. And all three shots came from behind, and all came from the same weapon fired by the same shooter. It was neat, clean and allowed the door to be slammed shut on any deviation."

"But the public didn't buy that, did they?" Ryan interjected. "So what was the Warren Commission to do?"

"That was a problem," Boggs agreed. "We were faced with a dilemma of sorts."

"Which was?"

"To depart from the FBI conclusions as laid out in their December 1963 report, the Warren Commission would have to take on the FBI and Mr. Hoover. And Warren was not going to allow that," Boggs revealed."

Ryan forged ahead, "But didn't you contradict the FBI report when you insisted that one of the three bullets fired caused seven wounds by striking two people, President Kennedy and Governor Connally?"

"Oh ya'," Boggs admitted. "The 'Single Bullet Theory' was a bit off the wall, wasn't it?"

"It certainly caused a big stir in the conspiracy community as well as the general public. It would have been more believable if you had just agreed with the FBI Report," Ryan told him.

Boggs agreed. "That's exactly what I said. Russell and Cooper thought so too. But you see, my friend, we had another problem; the FBI report that had the President struck by the first bullet, Connally the second, and JFK the third."

"What problem was that?"

"It couldn't be supported. Our May reenactment, tied in with the Zapruder film, made their finding untenable. That was the problem. Because it became obvious that a single shooter using the rifle recovered on the sixth floor of the Book Depository could not have hit the two men in the time shown on the Zapruder film. That's when Specter's 'single bullet theory' took on a life of its own. To contend otherwise meant we had to admit the existence of one or more additional shooters. But by the end of May, we had come to the end of our string," Boggs revealed. "We needed to finish up, and Specter's theory was all we had. It was either swallow hard and endorse the damn thing or admit that the assassination was a conspiracy involving others. That was a hornet's nest no one wanted to touch."

Ryan probed further. "So, for the sake of the country, you gave up your own objections, ignored eyewitness testimony and forensic evidence, and signed on to the commission's final report?"

"You got it, Harold. Understand now, I'm just speaking for myself when I tell you that Chief Justice Warren really leaned on the three of us to go along with the majority. He wanted all of us to endorse the lone shooter hypothesis and put the lid on any other possibility. He wanted to end the probe and not explore other possibilities. LBJ was pressing for an end, too. He didn't want to have to deal with unanswered questions during the fall presidential campaign."

"I see," Ryan said. "To end the investigation, Warren and President Johnson needed a unanimous decision from the panel?"

"Right, because if the commissioners were split, the question of who killed Kennedy would have been left unanswered. If that happened, both men argued, there would have been no end to the public outcry. And, the threat of thermonuclear war would have still hung out there just waiting for the first strong wind to blow us all up."

Ryan interrupted. "So, faced with those possibilities, you signed on?"

"Now you got it, buddy," Boggs admitted.

"Help me out here, Hale," Ryan begged. "How can I use what you've told me?"

"I don't rightly know, Harold. But if you need to use what you've heard today, it can't have come from me. You'll have to find another source."

"Thanks a lot, Hale."

On the way out the door, Boggs held Ryan back a moment. "Let me think about it, Harold," he said.

"Maybe I can come up with some way you can use what I told you."

"That would be much appreciated."

***

Meanwhile, Mike Burke drove to Havre de Grace, a Maryland area, to meet with Ronald Simmons. He was Chief of the Infantry Weapons Evaluation Branch of the Ballistics Research Laboratory of the Department of the Army.

"Thank you for meeting me out here at my place, Mr. Burke. I'd a' come into DC, but I've been having car trouble lately."

"It's quite all right," Mike responded, setting up his tape recorder in the small office.

"Could you describe the tests you ran for the Warren Commission, Mr. Simmons?"

"Certainly. I was asked to determine whether or not a rifleman using Oswald's rifle could duplicate the shots that killed President Kennedy and wounded Governor Connally."

"What were the conditions you set up?" Burke asked.

"Each of my three riflemen would fire three shots at stationary targets three different distances from the shooting platform; 175, 240, and 265 yards. They would use the rifle that had been identified as the weapon used by the assassin."

"Any other parameter involved?"

"Yes, there was, Mr. Burke," Simmons revealed. "The Commission wanted to see if three shots could be fired accurately from those distances in a time frame between 4.6 and 5.15 seconds."

"Who did the firing?"

"I recruited three men rated as Master Rifleman by the National Rifle Association. That's the highest rating that organization awards. Two of the men are gunners in the Small Arms Division of our Development and Proof Services. The third man is presently in the Army."

"What were the results?"

"Only one of the three men was able to get off three shots within the required period of time. The marksman, Miller, was able to do that during the first firing sequence at the target 175 feet away."

"As I recall, on November 22nd, 1963, the president was seated in a moving vehicle, correct?"

"Yes, sir, he was."

"But your master shooters were firing all three of their shots at fixed targets?"

"Yes, sir, that's correct."

"The window from which the assassin is said to have fired all three shots was 60 feet above the ground, but your master shooters were on a platform 30 feet above the ground."

"Yes, sir, that's true."

"I read one report of this test that said each of your master shooters was allowed to take all the time he wanted to fire his first shot while the assassin had less than one second to get off his first shot. Is this true?"

"Yes, sir, it is."

"Were any modifications made to the Italian rifle your master shooters used?"

"Yes, there were," Simmons revealed.

"What was done?"

"The technicians in my machine shop could not sight in the weapon using the telescopic sight attached to the rifle. So one of my machinists rebuilt that aiming device before my master shooters, as you call them, fired it for the test."

"Did any of your master shooters comment on the weapon?"

"You have to understand, Mr. Burke, that this was a very old rifle. So it shouldn't surprise anyone that one of my marksmen said that he had difficulty even opening the bolt. All three commented that the trigger pull was difficult."

***

Ryan was talking with Admiral George Burkley. The Admiral had been JFK's personal physician and was present in Dallas. He was also the only doctor present in both the Parkland Hospital trauma room and the Bethesda Hospital autopsy. He was also the physician who signed the death certificate in Dallas.

After the preliminaries were completed, Ryan went right to work.

"Admiral," he began. "In the course of the Bethesda autopsy, were you given a bullet taken from the president's body?"

"Yes, I was."

"Dr. Shaw told a New York Times reporter on November 27 that a bullet had entered the front of Kennedy's throat, coursed downward into his lung (and) was removed in the Bethesda Naval Hospital, where the autopsy was performed. Is Dr. Shaw talking about the bullet you were given?"

"I believe so, Mr. Ryan," Burkley said.

"What did you do with it, sir?"

"I turned it over to the FBI agents, Sibert and O'Neill, who were present in the autopsy room."

"Were you given a receipt by them?"

"Yes, I was."

"I assume you have that in your possession."

"Yes, I do."

"I'll need a copy of the original, sir."

"I'll think about it."

"I see. Is it true, sir," Ryan went on, "that during the autopsy, you stopped the doctors who were conducting the examination from cutting into the president's body to follow the paths taken by the bullets which struck him?"

"I had promised Mrs. Kennedy that her husband's body would not be mutilated."

"I'll take your answer to be a 'yes,'" Ryan snapped. "So you *did* prevent them from conducting a complete autopsy, did you not?"

Burkley's face reddened. "Yes. I did."

"So because of you, we will never know if President Kennedy was killed by a single crazed gunman or was the victim of a conspiracy. Is that how you want history to remember you, sir?"

"I don't care about that. I do care that I kept my promise to Mrs. Kennedy."

"Is it also true that you signed the president's death certificate while at Dallas's Parkland Hospital, sir?"

"Yes, I did."

"Do you have a copy of that in your possession?"

"Yes, I do."

"I will need a copy of that as well, sir."

"I'll consult my attorney about that, too."

"While you were in Trauma Room #1 at Parkland, did you observe the president's condition when he was first brought into the ER?"

"Yes, I did. "

"Did you see his throat wound before the doctors performed a tracheotomy?"

"Yes, I did."

"Was that wound an entry or exit wound, sir?"

"I couldn't tell."

"Describe the back wound, sir."

"I didn't examine it closely enough to describe it for you."

"Did you lie then, on the death certificate, sir?"

"Certainly not! In fact, it's insulting for you to even ask."

"Well, sir," Ryan said. "Either you answer my questions here in this quiet private room or before an investigating committee of the United States House of Representatives in the presence of the press and television cameras. The choice is yours, sir. So, Admiral," Ryan tried again. "Please describe the back wound suffered by President Kennedy."

The admiral paused for a few seconds, took a deep breath, and began his description.

"A bullet entered the president's back two inches or so to the right of the spine at the third thoracic vertebra, or about five inches down from his shirt collar. My measurements were verified by the holes in his coat and shirt. During the autopsy at Bethesda, Dr. Humes explored the back wound with his finger and determined that the bullet had entered the president's body at a downward angle of about 45 to 60 degrees."

Ryan then gave the Admiral a sketch illustrating the single bullet theory adopted by the Warren Commission.

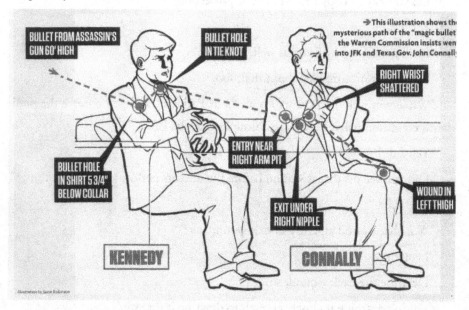

"Thank you, Admiral," Ryan said. "Could such a bullet traveling at such a downward angle have exited President Kennedy's body through the throat as suggested in this diagram?"

"Hardly," the admiral answered with a smirk. "And," he added, "my description of this wound was verified in a formal report made by the two FBI agents Sibert and O'Neill who were present at the Bethesda autopsy."

"When did you make your observations, sir?"

"My observation of the location of the back wound was made in the trauma room at Parkland Hospital. The angle of penetration was determined by Dr. Humes at Bethesda Hospital during the autopsy he performed there, which I witnessed."

"So, you identified the location of the back wound, and Dr. Humes discovered the angle of penetration?"

"Yes, that's true," Berkley agreed. "And, Mr. Ryan, I signed the autopsy fact sheet showing the location of the back wound just where I told you, five and a half inches down from the shirt collar and two inches to the right of the spine."

"Don't these two findings destroy the Warren Commission's contention that the very bullet we're talking about entered the president's body at the back of his neck, left by way of his throat, and entered the back of Governor Connally?"

"Yes, I'm aware of that." The Admiral agreed. "That's probably why I was never asked to testify for the Warren Commission."

"So, you can see that it could be rather important for us to know if that bullet is still in the president's body as the doctors at Parkland thought. You can see that, can't you?"

"Yes."

"But you stopped the doctors who were conducting the autopsy at Bethesda from opening the president's body in order to follow the path of that bullet, didn't you, Admiral?

"So, we'll never really know, will we?

"How do you think Mrs. Kennedy will feel when she finds out you prevented us from finding her husband's real killer, sir? For the Commission's final report, Congressman Ford had the location of the entry in the back changed to, 'A bullet had entered the base of the back of his neck slightly to the right of the spine.' Do you have any comment on this, sir?"

"It is not a correct identification of the wound I saw or the one described in the autopsy face sheet, which I verified with my signature."

"Do you have any other comments you wish to make, Admiral?" Ryan asked.

"Not at this time, Mr. Ryan."

Ryan stood. "Can we go to your office now, Admiral? I'd like to make a copy of both the death certificate and the receipt for that bullet you gave to the FBI over two years ago."

Harold Ryan returned to his office that afternoon with a copy of each document.

SILVER SPRING

Harold Ryan was at Mike's Maryland home this evening. They were going to spend some time with Marilyn on their scheduling needs and on their final report to the Committee on the Judiciary.

"Are you my dad's boss?" Ann asked in her usual straightforward manner.

Harold gave it right back to her. "What made you think I was his boss, Ann?"

"Because you have gray hair – you look older," she answered, not backing down at all.

"Don't be rude, Ann," her mother cautioned.

"That's quite all right, Mom," Harold assured her. "I have daughters of my own, you know. I like people who get right to the point with their questions.

"No, I'm not, Ann," he responded. "your dad and I just work together."

"Did you know that someone made my mom's car tires flat and that a dead cat was put on our porch?"

"Yes, your father told me."

"Why was that done?"

"I'm not sure why those things were done, Ann," Harold continued patiently. "Has anything like that happened since your dad returned home from his trip to Dallas?"

"I don't think so," Ann responded. "Mom, has anything bad happened around here since Dad got home?"

"Not that I know of, dear," she answered.

"Ya see?" Ryan concluded. "Probably was just a bad thing someone passing through thought would be a funny joke. Probably never happen again."

Satisfied for the moment, Ann returned to her Barbie dolls.

"Come on, everyone," Marilyn announced. "Supper's ready."

Mike lifted his youngest daughter Jackie into her high chair. Everyone else took a seat at the dining room table.

"Who is going to say grace tonight?" Mike asked.

"I will," Susan volunteered.

"Go ahead, Susan," her mother urged.

"Bless us o' Lord for these Thy gifts
And for what we are about to receive
We give Thee thanks."

"Amen," everyone said in unison.

"That was nicely done, Susan," Harold Ryan said. "You helped me feel right at home because we say that same prayer before dinner at my house, too."

Sue blushed some and said, "Thank you, Mr. Ryan."

After the meal, dishes were cleared, and the girls returned to their Barbie dolls. The adults sat around the table over cups of coffee.

Marilyn opened the discussion. "First, let's look over these lists." She passed out some paperwork.

"This is the list of names I've been working from when scheduling your appointments. Some of these people you have decided not to interview. A few, I discovered, have passed away, and others are just unavailable. You have already seen most of the rest. So, it would appear that you are pretty much done with interviews. Am I correct, or are there some other people you still need to see?"

Ryan responded first. "Don't forget, we still need to interview President Johnson, Arlan Specter, Lee Rankin, and Clint Hill before we can put together our report to the Judiciary Committee."

"I agree," Mike chimed in. "Of course, our meeting with Specter might lead us to see additional people, maybe not."

"Before you schedule these, Marilyn," Ryan interrupted. "I need to go over my personal schedule with you two."

"What's up, Harold?" Mike asked.

"I've got to head back to Detroit for a few days. I need to file for the Circuit Court race, go over things with members of my campaign team and confirm the endorsements I've been promised, and of course, raise some money."

"How long will you be gone?"

"Probably a week. I'll leave this Friday and return Sunday of the following week."

Mike told his wife, "That should be enough time for me to check out my leads on the suspected Zapruder film alterations and talk with Lee Rankin and Clint Hill. Harold and I have already decided to interview Specter and the president together."

"Before we go any further, though," Marilyn said. "let's get these three tired children tucked in for the night, Michael. Jackie has already fallen asleep on the floor."

"Come on, girls," their father announced. "Time for bath and bed."

"Oh, do we have to?" Ann complained.

"It's a school night," their mother reminded them.

Once the kids were washed up, they were in their jammies and in bed for the night. Mike skipped their nightly 'when he was a little boy' story.

Back at the table, Marilyn asked, "How does it look for you back in Detroit, Harold?"

"Pretty good, actually," he responded. "The Ryan name is like a magnet on the ballot. In fact, both white and black candidates with Irish names do very well in Wayne County elections. Getting the vote out in the August primary is the key. With so many names on the ballot, getting out your vote is crucial. That's why a good campaign organization is so necessary and in place before the primary election. I need to meet with the men and women who will take on that responsibility. It will help immensely that I'll be on the United Auto Worker's slate as well as the

AFL-CIO's recommended list. The Knights of Columbus will endorse me, too. If all these come through as promised, I should be fine. But a candidate can't take all that for granted. I need to nail it down; visit the people who control the endorsements, shake their hands, and remind them of their promises. I can't do that by phone, and I'll need about a week to get that done. Campaign ads are next. The TV and radio media, as well as the *Detroit News* and *Free Press* newspapers, will be crowded with political advertising leading up to the primary and before the fall voting. So when I'm back there next week, I also need to reserve some radio and TV time if I expect to have any ads playing during the last week of the fall campaign. Yard signs and campaign literature has to be ordered. I need to check on how that is going. If all of that wasn't enough, I need to raise some cash to pay for all this stuff. Detroit lawyers are always good for donations. But, there again, face-to-face is necessary."

"I wish there were something Mike and I could do to assist, Harold."

"I do too, Marilyn," Harold assured her. "Your help would certainly be appreciated. Maybe after we're done with this report, you'd visit Detroit and lend a hand."

"That sounds like it would be fun," Mike said. "We can talk about it when you return."

"In the meantime," Marilyn said, "It's back to work for you two."

"She's a real slave driver, Mike."

"Tell me about it."

"Get serious, you two, or I'll cut off your coffee supply. Here, take a look at what I've written up for you to review." She passed out a carbon copy of her originally typed sheet.

"I've stated the two primary objectives you told me about as the focus of your investigation.

"First: you set out to examine the basis for the single shooter theory. That meant you had to question the ability of one shooter to fire several times within a limited number of seconds at a moving target. And you had to examine the

Zapruder film frame by frame. You also decided to interview a sampling of witnesses who swore they heard shots from behind where they stood on the Grassy
Knoll and/or saw smoke from that area, too. Second: you intended to talk with
the medical people at Parkland to discover if they had changed their early opinions
that: the throat wound was an entry wound. The head wound was the result of a
shot to the front right of the president's head. Third: you intended to interview a
representative sample of people from the list of witnesses to the assassination about
what they saw/heard on Elm Street and the Grassy Knoll. So, my questions for
you are: Have you stayed true to these objectives? If you have, do you have enough
evidence to prove the assassination involved more than one shooter and was, therefore, a conspiracy?"

Both men remained quiet.

Harold spoke first. "Let me take your second question first, Marilyn. Every
doctor and nurse who spoke with me stood behind their earlier testimony that the
president had a throat wound that was inflicted from the front. And the two physicians who examined the president's head wound on November 22 still believe it
was also caused by a bullet hitting him from the front. All the descriptions they
gave me matched the notes they had made on November 22. There was no deviation."

Mike Burke spoke next. "I can address your first question, Marilyn. All those I
interviewed in Dallas insisted that bullets were fired from the Grassy Knoll to the
rear of where they were standing. A few of them even testified that a man with
Secret Service credentials waved them out of that area, too. None of this was in-
vestigated by local authorities, the FBI, or the Commission's staff."

"Also, the Commission employed three expert riflemen to reenact the assassination firing. Using the Italian-made rifle the Commission insisted had been the
murder weapon, these experts fired at a stationary target rather than a moving one.
Simmons, the man who set up those reenactments, admitted that none of his experts could repeat what Oswald was accused of doing within the timeline required,
even after other experts had improved the shaky telescopic sight that had been
mounted on the weapon."

Marilyn asked. "What about the Zapruder film?"

"What about it?"

"You still have to talk with some experts about the tampering issue?"

"I don't think so," Mike revealed. "Harold and I spent one of our Dallas evenings at Mr. Zapruder's home. He ran the film he took of the assassination for us."

"Several times, in fact," Harold added.

"We discovered two things," Mike continued. "First, that the *Life Magazine* story insisting that the president's throat wound was inflicted from the rear when he had turned far to his right to greet someone in the crowd was false. President Kennedy never turned far enough to his right for such a wound to have been inflicted from the Book Depository."

"That convinced Mike and me," Harold said, "that the Parkland doctors were right. They were correct when they insisted that the president's throat wound resulted from a shot from the front of the motorcade. And secondly," he said, "we clearly saw that the head wound that killed the president did not come from the rear. It was quite the reverse. Zapruder's film showed the president's head snapping back, not forward as it seemed to in *Life Magazine's* printed version."

Mike concluded, "The film he showed us was conclusive as far as I'm concerned."

"I'd be comfortable showing that in court to support our claim that two shots hit the president from the front; the throat wound and the killing head wound." Harold insisted.

"That's good enough for me, too." Mike finished.

"I'll cross that one off the list then," Marilyn told them.

"Well, gentlemen," Marilyn concluded. "It appears to me that you have accomplished the two goals you set for your investigation. So, why do either of you need to interview anyone else? "

"Aside from President Johnson, Arlan Specter, Lee Rankin, and Clint Hill, you mean, Marilyn?" Harold asked.

"Right," she answered.

"Those four should do it, seems ta' me," Mike told them.

"Maybe you're right, Mike. But, before we congratulate ourselves on a job well done, let's take some time and see if we have enough testimony and data to prove our case." Ryan cautioned.

"I think I'm hearing the lawyer talking, Marilyn," Mike told his wife.

"So, what's troubling you, Harold?" Marilyn asked.

"I have some thoughts sort of nagging at me about the quality of the testimony we've taken. But it's pretty late tonight, and I'm dead tired. I think we should tackle this in the morning. Let's go over everything we've collected then and see where we stand."

Marilyn stood. "I'm for that. How about you, Michael?"

"The morning is fine with me."

"Super," Marilyn concluded. "Let me show you the guest room, Harold."

WASHINGTON, D.C.

Ryan had been gone since the previous Friday. Burke had visited Lee Rankin in New York City on Tuesday morning.

On his return to Washington that afternoon, he was scheduled to visit with Secret Service agent Clinton Hill. On trips with President Kennedy and his wife, Hill's assignment had usually been to provide security for Mrs. Kennedy.

During the Dallas motorcade, he had been riding on the left running board of the Secret Service follow-up car directly behind JFK's limo. According to his Warren Commission testimony, Hill left the follow-up car and ran forward to the presidential vehicle as soon as he heard the first shot. He testified, " … the second shot I heard had removed a portion of the president's head, and he slumped noticeably to his left."

"How in heaven's name could you catch up to a vehicle traveling at a normal motorcade speed of eleven or so miles per hour?" Burke asked.

"Because the president's limo had virtually stopped after the first shot."

"That seems weird," Burke said. "Shouldn't the driver have sped away from the area at the sound of the first shot?"

"You would think, Mr. Burke," Hill admitted. "All I know is that the driver of the president's limo stopped the vehicle."

"According to your testimony, you got a good look at the head injury. Is that true?"

"Yes, sir," he said. "I'll never forget the image of the president's head wound. I wish I could stop remembering it, Mr. Burke. Mr. Kennedy was leaning on Mrs. Kennedy. His head was almost on her lap, and I was right above her. So, I saw his head wound real close; I've not been able to get that image out of my mind. Part of the skull was gone… his brain was exposed… one large gaping wound in the right rear portion of his head."

"And you were present at Parkland Memorial in the trauma room?"

"Yes, sir, I was," Hill answered. "I stayed because Mrs. Kennedy wouldn't leave him, ya see. So, I couldn't leave her. Watching what they were doing to his body was worse than seeing what happened out on Elm Street. At least the shooting was over in a few seconds."

"Then you stayed with the president's body on the flight to Washington and when it was taken to Bethesda Hospital?"

"Yes, sir, I did," Hill said. "At first, I was there to be with Mrs. Kennedy on the flight back to Washington. I didn't want her to be alone. But after we got back there, Robert Kennedy was with her. Then, I didn't want President Kennedy to be alone. So I joined Admiral Burkley and watched the autopsy at Bethesda Naval Hospital."

"Did you see the head wound again?"

"Yes, sir, I did," Hill said. "By now, the president's head wound was cleaned up some; not so much blood and brain matter around. I was surprised by the large size of the opening on the back right of his head. An' this time, I saw part of his brain just lying there on the table. It was terrible for me to see him like that," Hill said. "He had been so respectful of me and the other Secret Service guys assigned to him and his family. He was so full of life. I think he would have been a great president. Admiral Burkley stopped the doctors from cutting up the president's body, searching for bullets. He said he had promised Mrs. Kennedy he wouldn't let them do that."

"Do you have anything more to add, Mr. Hill?"

"No, sir," he said. "I've never been part of something so awful, Mr. Burke. An' I hope I never am again."

"I agree, Mr. Hill. Thank you for coming in."

DETROIT

Harold Ryan walked into the entrance of the United Auto Workers' offices located on Jefferson Avenue. He went right to the third-floor offices of Sam Fishman. Fishman directed the political activities of the union.

"Good morning, Congressman Ryan," Sam's secretary greeted.

This lady has a knack for remembering everybody's name. It's a gift I envy.

"Can I get you a coffee or some juice?"

"Coffee, black, would be fine, Alice," he answered.

"Mr. Fishman is expecting you, sir."

Harold took his cup of coffee and looked around the reception area at all the photographs on the walls. *There must be a personalized photo of every Democratic Michigan politician and a few from outside the state on these walls,* he thought. *I see my photo is still up there. I look very distinguished standing by my desk in the House Chamber. That title still has a nice ring to it. That's all in the past, though. Now, Circuit Court Judge sounds just fine. That's my present and future, I hope.*

"Mr. Fishman will be with you shortly, Congressman," Alice assured him.

In less than a minute, the door to his office opened, and Harold's host hurried out. Full of energy and with a big smile, Sam extended his hand to Harold. You'd think Sam was selling something, instead of Harold.

"Great to see you, Harold," he almost shouted. "Come on in. Bring your coffee with you. Need it freshened?"

"No, Sam," Harold assured him. "I'm fine. You're not having any?"

"My heart doctor has ordered me not to drink the stuff. Says it's not good for me. He took cigars away from me, too. At least I can have sex once in a while. My wife controls that, though."

They both laughed at that one.

"I know what you mean, Sam," Harold agreed. "Sometimes I think all the fun stuff is either bad for us or beyond our capacity."

"You got that right, my friend," Sam said. "How is the Washington thing coming along?"

"You know about that, do you?"

"Sure," Sam revealed. "John Conyers asked for my opinion before he called you."

"I figured you had a hand in my appointment. Thanks for the recommendation."

"You've been around the political block a few times, Harold. You know how the game is played. I told him you were one of our guys and that you were a team player."

"Thanks, Sam, I appreciate it," Harold assured him.

"I heard that some overzealous FBI agent took a shot at you and your partner while you were in Dallas. How crazy is that?"

"Real crazy, Sam. All it did, aside from scaring the shit out of me, was to get Conyers real mad. He told us to go after the truth wherever it took us."

"Will you?" Sam asked.

"Actually, it's Conyer's call," Harold assured him. "Whatever he decides to do with the information our report provides, I believe the truth will show that those bastards in Washington pulled a crude cover-up after the assassination."

"Just you be careful, my friend. I'd hate you to be the one blamed for bringing down LBJ and handing the presidency over to the Republicans in next year's election. If there's any heat to be taken for damaging our chances in '68, let Conyers take it."

"You're right, Sam, as usual. Thanks for the heads-up. I'll be careful. Now, about my race for Circuit Judge," Harold asked. "Are you still going to support me?"

"I told you I would, Harold," Sam reminded him. "You will be endorsed by the United Auto Workers for a seat on the Circuit Court. You're one of our guys. You've earned our support, and I intend to tell our membership that. "

Then, he called Alice into the room. "Alice, will you take notes of our meeting. Please?"

Sam continued to answer Harold's initial question.

"Our union's slate will have your name on it. Every working member and re- tiree who lives in Wayne County will get a copy of that list and will be urged to support every candidate listed. On Election Day, our poll workers will hand out copies of that list at every voting place in Wayne County."

"That sounds great, Sam. How many additional copies of that list can my peo- ple have?"

"You can have as many as you want for your workers to pass out."

"Great. Who'll be my contact with your office?"

"Harold," Sam said, leaning forward in his chair, "you can always call me di- rectly. Alice, I want you to put Harold's calls through any time."

"Yes, sir." She responded. "I'll remember that."

"But I've appointed Jimmy George to coordinate your campaign. He'll be the one you and your workers should work with. Have you got anyone heading up your effort?"

"Jim Killeen will be my campaign chairman," Harold responded. "He's already got some folks to recruit workers at the precinct level."

"Good choice. I worked with Jim in the past and know him well. Bill Marshal, president of the Michigan AFL-CIO, has promised to help with his union's get- out-the-vote effort for the primary and the final election. My contact guy with him is Paul Seldonright."

"That's great. How about Wayne County AFL-CIO president Tom Turner? Is he on board?"

"I'm not completely sure. But Marshal has set up a meeting for me with him later this week."

"That's super," Sam told Harold. "You've got to have Tom on board if you hope to get the Black vote. I'll put in a call to him and let him know of our endorsement. Remind me, Alice."

"Yes, sir," she responded.

"Which brings me to ask, how do you stand with the Black Minister's Association?"

"I'm a little weak on that front. Do you have any suggestions?"

"Yes, I do," Sam revealed. "I've got a meeting coming up with the church leaders. Getting their pulpit support was easier when you were a Congressman. Then, they wanted you to vote for federal money to fund the Head Start and Pre-School programs they ran out of their churches. It's a bit harder now for them to see what benefit a circuit judge will be to their community. But, they usually support the union and Democratic Party slates as a package. I don't have any reason to believe that will change this political cycle."

"How about yard signs and media, Sam?" Harold asked. "What can you do for me there?"

"I can help you with some of the printed material, but the TV and radio stuff, you'll have to finance on your own. For the printed stuff like yard signs and brochures, I suggest you work with Splane Printers. Alice, please call Jack Splane and tell him to send me the cost estimate for Harold's campaign."

"Yes, sir."

" Harold, just don't go overboard on that stuff. My pockets are not that deep for the primary. But I'll do what I can. Work with me on this part. OK?"

"Right. I appreciate your help, believe me, Sam."

"You have any other organizations lined up?"

"As a matter of fact, I do. The Knights of Columbus are going to endorse me. And Killeen has set up a meeting with Ed Farhat of the Michigan Catholic Conference. I hope they'll get their people out for me, too."

"Sounds good, Harold," Sam concluded. "You've got some solid things going. I hate to cut this short, but I've got to get to another meeting right now. Please check in with Alice once a week. I don't want to have to chase you around if I need to talk with you. From time to time, get her your schedule as well. Oh, ya, give her your phone numbers before you leave today. She has a folder for you with all our phone numbers you'll need. Jimmy George will be expecting your call today, too. If you delay calling him, I suspect he'll take that as disrespect, and you'll have problems you don't need. Be sure to call him today. Understand, Harold?"

"Yes, I hear what you're saying, Sam."

"Another tip when dealing with Jimmy; ask him about his family, especially his wife. In fact, invite them to your home for supper. That kind of thing is important to him. And he is important to your campaign. Got me?"

Harold smiled. "I got it, Sam."

"By the way, Sam," Harold asked. "I almost forgot to mention it. Can you get some released time, or whatever you call it, for someone to work with me the last couple of weeks before the primary? He would also act as my driver and take me to meetings in the black community."

"You have someone in mind?"

"Yes. He's a fellow who I got to know on my last Congressional campaign. He works at the Chrysler plant in Hamtramck, name of Gonzalee Sullivan III. He's a well-spoken, neatly-dressed family man who is an experienced campaign worker. He's a hard worker, too. In fact, he'll have his undergrad degree from Wayne State University next year."

"I'll check it out, Harold, and get back to you. Give Alice all his information. All right?"

"Gotta run."

Such is the nature of politics in Detroit, Harold thought.

***

Now, Harold had a lunch appointment with Jim Killeen. The UAW Headquarters was right down Jefferson Avenue from the Federal Immigration office where Jim was a supervisor.

That was only ten minutes at most away, especially since they were meeting at Joe Muir's Restaurant. More deals were probably struck at the tables there than in the Detroit mayor's office. Over his years in Michigan politics, Harold had eaten there often.

When he walked in the door, the receptionist greeted him.

"Good afternoon, Congressman. Mr. Killeen is already here. If you follow me, I'll take you to his table."

"Thank you."

As they approached, Jim stood to greet Harold.

"Good to see you, Judge," he exclaimed while pumping Harold's hand. "How did your meeting with Sam go?"

"Excellent. It couldn't have gone any better. He is solid, and so is the UAW."

"That's great news."

"In fact, he is going to pick up the cost of yard signs and brochures for our precinct workers."

"I knew you could do it, Harold," Jim congratulated his candidate. "I knew you could do it."

"Sam was impressed that the Michigan Catholic Conference and the Knights of Columbus are going to help."

"Along that line, you have a lunch appointment with Ed Farhat on Wednesday at the Peninsular Club in Lansing. You're to meet him in his office first, at 11 a.m. Then he'll take you to lunch with a few members of the House Black Caucus. I've got Joe Mancinelli taking a day off from his Detroit fireman's job to drive you. He'll also photograph you with members of the Black Caucus. And, you're to tape record short endorsements from each of them for our use during the primary on the Detroit radio stations that cater to the black community. Joe will help you with that, too. I've got the copy for those ten-second spots in this folder."

"Wow!" Harold exclaimed. "You've really got things going, Jim. Have you picked out my wardrobe, too?"

"Now that you mention it, Harold, please wear a blue suit with a white dress shirt and a red tie for this meeting."

Both men laughed heartily.

"Following lunch, Farhat will take you to a meeting with Bill Marshal at the AFL-CIO offices. You're to have a conversation with him just like the one you had this morning with Sam Fishman. I need you to put the squeeze on him to pick up the cost for the Detroit radio spots on the black radio stations. Try not to let him push you to get Tom Turner to pay for them. We need Tom to host a dinner for the members of Detroit's ministerial association. OK, Harold?"

Harold was taking notes, mental ones.

"Got it," he assured his campaign director. "What about copy for yard signs and brochures for the printer?"

"I've got Joe Yager working on that. He'll get that stuff to the printer. Joe is going to be our contact with Paul Donahue, Nedzi's Detroit office manager. They are old friends and have worked on political campaigns together in the past. Have you arranged to see your old buddy Lucian Nedzi yet?" Killeen asked.

"I'm meeting with him and Donahue tomorrow."

Killeen interrupted. "Good, and don't hesitate to promise him that you will never go after his seat in Congress as long as he holds it. We need his help with the voters in Hamtramck," he reminded Harold. "Ask Donahue to organize a lunch for the wives of the Hamtramck firefighters and the police officer wives. Remember, those women control the voting places in that city."

"How can I forget their role in my 1964 primary campaign against their man Nedzi? He had conceded the election to me around midnight. Remember that? But, around 5 a.m., a ballot box mysteriously showed up from Hamtramck. The paper ballots in that box took the election away from me and gave it to Nedzi. That was a nightmare I'll never forget."

"Don't forget, Harold. I was there, too. Go easy with him and Donahue." Jim cautioned. "We need their support in Hamtramck."

"Don't worry, Jim," Harold assured him. "I'll be sweet and soft-spoken. With the UAW endorsement in my pocket, they should be cooperative. If they prove to be reluctant, I'll have Fishman call the Congressman personally."

And, so the week went for Harold Ryan. His pre-election work in Detroit occupied his days as well as his evenings: one meeting after another.

He hadn't completely forgotten Mike Burke and their work in Washington, though.

I'd best give Mike a call, at least to let him know I'm still alive.

SILVER SPRING

"Good evening, Marilyn," Harold greeted. "How are you and the girls?"

"We're doing just fine, Harold. How is your campaign trip going?"

"Really good, thank you. I'll tell you about it when I see you next week."

"I look forward to that. Want to talk to Michael?"

"You bet."

"Michael," his wife called. "Harold is on the phone for you."

Mike took the phone. "It's about time you let us know you're alive. How is everything going?"

"Couldn't be better, Mike. I've spent my days listening to labor leaders tell me how much they think of me and pledging their full support. My evenings are spent at political meetings listening to promises of help. It could go to a guy's head."

"Oh, my Lord," Mike exclaimed. "Will I have to bow and kiss your ring when you return?"

"It hasn't gone quite that far, Mike. But, a little more respect from you might be in order."

"I don't want to hear this." Mike moaned. "When can you get back here?"

"I think I'm right on schedule, Mike," Harold assured him. "I should be in the office first thing Monday. What have you got lined up?"

"Two big ones, my friend," Mike challenged. "First, we go to Philadelphia for a long interview with Arlan Specter. Then, we interview President Johnson."

"I'm surprised the president agreed to see us."

"Conyers arranged that one."

Mike continued. "First thing Monday, we need to put together our questions for each of these guys. We only have this one shot with these two. So, I'll arrange to have Marilyn in the office on Monday to help us."

"I'm happy to hear she'll be there," Harold assured Mike. "I still have that list of questions for Specter she put together for us before I left town. I'll go over it when I get a minute. I think it might be wise for you to arrange for a stenographer to work with us that day, too."

"Good idea, Harold. Anything else you can think of?"

"Not right now, but I gotta' tell you, Mike, there's a ton of work for you and Marilyn to do on my campaign in Detroit. I'm swamped. I could sure use your help here."

"Good to hear that we'd be welcome, Harold. We'll talk about it and share with you next week."

"All right," Ryan concluded. "If I think of anything else, I'll call you. In any case, I'll see you next Monday morning. First one in the office makes the coffee, all right?"

"You got it. Take care."

"You think Harold will beat us into the office this morning?" Marilyn asked.

"I'll bet a lunch on it," Mike answered. "He called last night to tell us he was in town. And, based on past performance, he'll be waiting for us to arrive and have coffee made to boot."

"We'll see," Marilyn mused.

Sure enough, Harold was sitting at his desk enjoying a cup of coffee.

"'Bout time you two showed up," he quipped. "We're wasting daylight here, don't ya' know."

He stood and gave Marilyn a hug and shook Mike's hand.

"You don't look any worse for wear, Harold," Mike observed. "Campaigning seems to agree with you."

"Keeps my weight down, that's for sure. Get yourself some coffee and bring me up to date on what's happened while I was gone."

Mike reviewed his interview with Hill first. Then he told Harold and Marilyn about his trip to New York City to see Lee Rankin.

"Rankin was interesting," Mike began. "I asked him how they determined the number of shots fired that day. He replied, "The FBI Report stated that three shots were fired, all from behind the president by a single shooter. They found three shell casings in the Book Depository sniper's nest to support that claim. Rankin also said that Hoover or somebody at the Bureau leaked that report to the press before the Commission staff had even moved into their Washington offices."

"So," he continued, "Chief Justice Warren was initially inclined to live with the three-shot scenario Hoover claimed had been fired; one hitting President Kennedy in the back, a second shot wounding Governor Connally, and a third shot hitting the president's head and killing him. But, as the Commission staff began to collect the physical evidence, that conclusion began to appear shaky. The Zapruder film, eyewitness testimony, the Tague bullet, and the limo windshield damage considered together began to cast doubt on the FBI findings. So, Rankin added, 'Specter told the Commission members that there was either another shooter or a single bullet hit the president in the back, another hit him in the neck, exited by way of his throat, and wounded Connally. Thus, the Commission chose to avoid looking into the possibility of additional shooters and instead adopted the single bullet theory, the one we have called 'the magic bullet theory.''

Harold asked. "What did Rankin say about the three members of the Commission who didn't believe the single bullet theory?"

"He admitted that Boggs, Russell, and Cooper refused to go along with that explanation. They only agreed to sign the final report if their reluctance was noted in the report."

"But, there is no such explanation shown in the report," Marilyn protested. "Looking at the report, one would think all the members of the Commission agreed to its findings. How did he explain that?"

Mike chuckled. "He said it was a mystery to him. Somehow their reservations were omitted from the final report that was printed and made public."

"That's it?" Marilyn asked.

"Yep," Mike told her. "He sat in front of me cold stone sober."

"Didn't even one of the three men protest?" Harold asked.

"Rankin said that all three men were angry about it. But, they realized that raising a stink would cast doubt on the entire report. So, they all kept quiet."

"Incredible," Marilyn said. "Earl Warren, the Chief Justice of the Supreme Court, who is the most respected jurist in the United States, ignored the evidence and lied. That's enough to piss off a saint," she spat.

Harold added, "And Hoover, the most respected crime fighter in the country, led the way."

"Harold," Mike asked, "do you think we have enough evidence for the Judiciary Committee to believe what you and Marilyn have just said?"

"Before I answer that question," Harold said. "Let's go over our notes in each category.

"Where do you want to start?" Marilyn asked, fishing through folders filled with notes.

"Let's take the Grassy Knoll witnesses first," Mike said.

After looking through the notes Mike took from witnesses, Marilyn said, "You have interviewed twelve people who swear one or more shots came from the Grassy Knoll area. That's out of over fifty people who gave such testimony to local police, the FBI, the Warren Commission, or the Dallas sheriff's deputies. Is twelve enough, Harold?"

"Yes: it certainly is enough to warrant a thorough investigation of the possibility that one or more shots came from that area."

"But there was no such investigation. What does that say?" Marilyn persisted.

"It says to most fair-minded people that something was very wrong with both the FBI and the Warren Commission investigations."

"And, don't forget," Mike reminded them, "there were some people riding in the motorcade who smelled gun smoke coming from the Grassy Knoll, too. That latter group included U.S. Senator Yarborough, Mrs. Earle Cabell, the wife of the Dallas mayor, and U.S. Congressman Ray Roberts."

Mike added, "West and Breneman were the men who designed and supervised all the reenactments for *Time-Life* and the government. They told me their studies revealed that one person shooting from the Book Depository could not have fired all the verified shots. And, I suggest that my interview with Mr. Simmons clinches it. He's the ballistics expert who recruited and supervised the three expert shooters who failed in their attempts to duplicate what Oswald is said to have done, and this was at a stationary target, not a moving one. Not one of them hit the head or neck of the stationary targets in eighteen tries. Only one of them managed to get off three shots within the time shown in the Zapruder film. "

Mike continued, "Add to that the testimony of an FBI weapons expert, Agent Robert A. Frazier. Under questioning by Warren Commission attorneys, he revealed that once he stabilized the scope, he could fire Oswald's weapon three times in 4.6 seconds 25 yards away from a stationary target and achieve a three-inch spread of hits. At 100 yards, he believed he could hit three times within a 12-inch circle. When pressed, Frazier admitted that he would have to add one second per shot if he were firing at a moving target. At 3.3 seconds per round, for a total of 6.6 seconds, Frazier would not have been able to fire three shots in the window of time the Commission claimed the shooter had on November 22nd. Surprisingly, the Commission chose the fastest possible time of 2.3 seconds per shot and ignored the additional second per round Frazier said he would need if his target was moving."

"Are you finished, Michael?" Marilyn asked.

"For now, I am."

She turned to Harold. "What about the medical evidence?" she asked.

"I believe the testimony from the Parkland ER professionals is really striking and conclusive. My notes show clearly that the throat wound was one of entry. We have unimpeachable eyewitness testimony from credible professionals to support that conclusion. These witnesses based their determination on their examination of President Kennedy in the Parkland ER room and announced it publicly at a press conference before it was decided in Washington that all the shots had to have come from behind the motorcade."

He added, "My list of witnesses in Dallas includes Dr. Carrico, Dr. Baxter, Dr. Jenkins, Dr. Peters, Dr. Jones, Dr. Perry, and Nurse Henchcilffe. All of them reported a small wound the size of a pencil eraser in the front of the throat and identified it as an entry wound. They found no exit wound. Once we prove that the throat wound was one of entry, that means it was inflicted by a bullet fired from the front of the motorcade. The FBI Report and the Warren Commission Report insist that all shots were fired from behind the motorcade. So their reports would be blown clear out of the water."

"What about the head wound, though?" Marilyn asked.

"Doesn't really matter, Marilyn," Harold insisted. "Think about it. If the throat wound came from the front, there had to be a second shooter. It's as simple as that. But even in the case of the fatal head wound, both the FBI Report and the

Warren Commission Report are challenged by eyewitness testimony that places an exit wound at the back of the head, not the front. Such testimony has the kill shot hitting the president from the right front. That shot, by the way, brings us back to the Grassy Knoll as its source."

"Convinces me, Harold," Marilyn said with a smile. "But is it enough for Conyers and his Judiciary Committee?"

"I believe that if we were facing a panel or a jury made up of randomly selected Americans," Harold began. "I'd say they would, at the very least, decide that both reports were poorly supported by the available evidence. But I'm convinced that such a jury would decide that both reports were poor attempts at covering up how President Kennedy was actually assassinated."

"How about the Zapruder film?" Marilyn asked. "Does that fit in here someplace?"

"How do you see that, Mike?" Harold asked.

"While you were gone, I talked to two of the three experts who ran studies on the film. One of the three hasn't gotten back to me. Anyway, two of the studies clearly show that frames had been removed to allow support for the single bullet theory. I expect a summary of each study to arrive by mail any day. These guys promised that their summary would explain the whole thing."

"I hope so, Mike," Harold chuckled. "I sure don't understand that whole business."

"That may be true for all of us, Harold." Mike agreed. "But, I think it important that we are ready to show how the Commission staff used film with frames edited out in order to support their single shooter decision."

Harold wasn't convinced. "Doesn't that just get us mired down into all kinds of technical jibber-jabber and detract from our argument concerning the directionality of the shots?" he asked.

"It could," Mike admitted, "So, let's write up our case first. If we decide our case is strengthened by including the Zapruder tampering material, fine; if not, we leave it out."

"You're beginning to sound like a lawyer already, Mike," Harold said.

Marilyn picked up on that remark, "Where did that comment come from, Harold?"

"I'll tell you when we get to discussing my Circuit Court campaign, Marilyn. OK?"

"All right, you two," Marilyn concluded. "You'd best get yourselves organized for your interview with the President and the one with Arlan Specter. I suggest we review your questions for them before we leave the office today."

"Is she always this pushy, Mike?" Harold asked.

"Yep. She gets her way most of the time, too."

OFFICES OF THE PRESIDENT OF THE UNITED STATES

The president's appointment secretary, Bill Moyers, had Burke and Ryan in his office before their interview with President Johnson.

"I want you two to understand something," he began sternly. "You're here as a favor to Congressman Conyers. He asked the president to see you. You have fifteen minutes; that's all. Be ready to stand and leave when I open that door. Do I make myself clear?"

Mike's face colored slightly, and he asked, "Do we crawl on our hands and knees too?"

Moyers jumped up, face beet red. "What did you say?"

Burke smiled and replied, "By the look on your face, Mr. Moyers, I believe you heard me clearly. You can open that door whenever you want," Mike continued, "But if the president is answering one of our questions, I don't intend to stand or interrupt him in any way. We might be here because Congressman Conyers asked the president to see us. But President Johnson could use something from us, too. In Vietnam, he's waist-deep in alligators. He could use what we can give him; a clean report card on the killing of John Kennedy."

Mike concluded. "We'll leave the hallowed presence when he tells us, not you."

Moyers stood there stunned. He was not used to being talked to like this. He turned and told Ryan and Burke, "Please follow me."

After the introductions were completed, Burke and Ryan were seated across from the president, who remained behind a massive desk.

"Didn't I campaign with you in Detroit back in '64, Harold?" President Johnson asked.

"Yes, sir. You and I worked the Chrysler Plant gate on Jefferson Avenue at 5 a.m.," Harold reminded him. "Then we had an early breakfast at a church, the New Mount Hope Missionary Baptist Church. That was followed by a visit to the

Parke Davis plant, where we said hello to the ladies coming into work later that morning. At that point, Mr. President, I was exhausted," Harold revealed. "But, you went on for what I assume was a full schedule."

Seasoned campaigners, both men were chuckling now.

"Sounds about right, Harold," Johnson agreed. "I hear you're running for circuit judge back in Detroit."

"Yes, sir. I am."

"Good luck with that. I appreciate your willingness to take the time out of your campaign for this project. We need to assure the people of our country that the FBI Report and the Warren Commission Report were both solid. If I can help toward that end by answering a few questions, let's get to it."

Burke went first.

"The United Press International ran a story on November 22, 1963. It was based on an interview with Vice President Nixon. In the course of the interview, he said you had become, and I quote, "a political liability in both the North and the South, and therefore might be dropped from the 1964 Kennedy reelection ticket. Was there any truth to that story, sir?"

"Y'all haf ta' remember, Nixon's a Republican. An' I expect he'll be a candidate for president in '68. A' course he would say things like that. It's part of the political game, don't ya' know."

"No truth to it then, sir?"

"Beats me, son," the president added. "What's next?"

"Word around town in the spring of 1963 was that you would be involved with Bobby Baker and Billy Sol Estes in scandals that could end your political career. Care to comment on that, sir?" Harold asked.

"As you know, Mr. Baker is serving time in a federal prison for influence peddling, among other things. As you see, I have not been linked to that type of thing. Don't you think my enemies would have been happy to do so if there was any chance they could make the charge stick?"

Harold Ryan asked this question.

"A Texas lady, a Mrs. Brown, quotes you as saying on the evening of November 21, 1963, 'After tomorrow, those Kennedys will never embarrass me again.' Did you say that, sir?"

"I don't recall talking with a Mrs. Brown that evening. An' I certainly don't think I'd say something as foolish as that."

Burke followed, "Sir, do you think the killing of President Kennedy was a conspiracy or the act of a lone killer?"

"Ya, know, young fella," the president began, "I've given that some serious thought. With all the contrary evidence that's come out since the two reports, I'd have ta' say there's a pretty good case to be made for more than one shooter."

"Do we have time for one more, sir?" Harold asked.

"Sure nuff," the president replied. "What is it?"

"It has been verified that President Kennedy issued the National Security Action Memorandum # 263 in October of 1963 ordering the accelerated withdrawal of all American advisors from Vietnam to be completed by 1965, starting with 1,000 by the end of 1963. Is it true, sir, that you countermanded that order with Memorandum # 273, on November 24, 1963, just two days after the assassination of President Kennedy?"

"Yes, I did," Johnson replied without hesitation. "The late president and I differed on what our position should be in Vietnam. I believed, and I still believe, we have to help our allies fight Communist aggression wherever and whenever it takes place. It appears that President Kennedy was somewhat selective and excluded Vietnam from that obligation. I did not."

Bill Moyers came into the room and announced, "Sir," he told the president, "you're due to meet with the Secretary of Defense in the Situation Room."

"Hear that?" Johnson moaned, standing up. "As y'all can see, my time is not my own any more. Good to see you again, Harold. Good luck on your campaign."

"Thank you, sir," Harold said, shaking the president's hand. Johnson did not extend his hand to Burke.

Another door opened mysteriously, and the president of the United States strode out of the room.

SILVER SPRING

Mike was home today before the kids had their supper.

"Hi, Dad," Susan said. She and Jackie were in the downstairs tub taking a bath.

"Hi, girls," he greeted. After he gave them each a hug, he asked. "Little early for your bath, isn't it? Where's Ann?"

Jackie said, "We were all full of sand, so Mom told us we had to wash up before dinner. She's having a time-out in the guest bedroom."

"Ann's having a time-out in the guest bedroom," Susan told her father.

"Why?" Mike asked.

"She dumped a bucket full of sand all over David Miles this afternoon." Susan continued.

"She socked him, too," Jackie added.

"Why?" Mike asked again.

"He's a real creep, Dad," Susan said. "We were all playing in their new sandbox. Mom and Mrs. Miles were sitting on their back porch talking. And for no good reason, David pushed Jackie down and then dumped a bucket full of sand all over her."

"Then what happened?"

"Ann grabbed him by his shirt and socked him right in the face. He fell down crying, the big baby, and then she filled a bucket full of sand and dumped it all over him."

That's my girl. Sounds like something her mother would have done, too.

"What did Mom do?"

By this time, Marilyn had come into the bathroom.

"Mom took your daughter home, gave her a swat on her bottom, and put her in the front bedroom to think about her unladylike behavior."

DID OSWALD ACT ALONE?

"Would you mind if I talked to my daughter, Mom?" Mike asked

"Go right ahead, Michael. I tried, but she insists the little snot had it coming for hitting her sister."

"He's a little bully, Mom," Susan stated. "He didn't pick on me or Ann. He knows we wouldn't put up with it. No, he picked on little Jackie. If Ann hadn't knocked him down, I would have. She just beat me to it, is all."

"Now he knows what will happen to him when he picks on one of the Burke girls," Susan concluded.

Mike wanted to cheer. The girl's mother was stunned at the outburst.

Mike hid his smile behind his hand as he turned away and went into the guest bedroom. "I think I'll talk with Ann."

She was lying on the bed. "Hi, kiddo," he greeted and sat beside her. "Got a hug for your dad?"

"Are you mad at me too, Dad?" Ann asked.

"I love you too much to be mad at you," Mike assured his daughter. "But it will be easier for me if you explain what happened today. Would you do that, sweetheart?"

Ann sat up. "Sure, Dad, I can do that," she said. She began telling him what happened.

"Mrs. Miles called Mom and invited us all over to play with her boys in their new sandbox. So, we went. We were playing sandcastles and cars in the sand. Mom sat with Mrs. Miles on their back porch. Everything was going along just swell when suddenly David punched Jackie in her chest. She fell out of the sandbox onto the driveway and started crying. If that wasn't bad enough, David dumped a pail full of sand on her, too."

"You and Susan were still in the sandbox with the other two Miles boys. Right?"

"Yes. But not for long. Susan jumped out to help Jackie. And I stood up and looked over at Mrs. Miles. She was just sitting there as though nothing was wrong. I suppose she was used to her son acting like a jerk. So I socked David good and hard. He fell out of the sandbox onto the cement driveway. It was only when he started crying that his mother paid any attention."

"What did she do?"

"She stood up and shouted, 'Who pushed David?'"

"And, what did Ann Burke do then?"

"That made me so mad, Dad," Ann sputtered. "I'm still mad that she didn't care about what her bully son did to my little sister. But she only cared about what I did to him. So, I dumped a bucket of sand on him, just like he did to Jackie."

"Does sound fair to me," Mike admitted.

"Well, tell that to Mom. You notice that I'm the one being punished. I just looked out the window at that jerk, David Miles, playing out in front of his house. He's not being punished for starting the whole thing."

"Your mom and I are not concerned with what his parents do when he acts like he just did, sweetheart. We are concerned that you and your sisters act properly however you are tempted."

"But you said what I did, sounded fair to you."

"It still does, Ann," her father was quick to tell her, "but I hope you will consider a less violent response to such bad behavior in the future."

Hearing that, Ann sat up straight, gave him her best challenge look, reconsidered, and said, "What should I have done then, Dad?"

This little girl is learning how to handle her ol' man, I see.

"How about this, sweetheart?" Mike responded, "First, you might have helped Susan look after Jackie. Then, the three of you could have gone to your mom and told her that the Miles boys were not playing nicely. And, because of their bad behavior, you all wanted to go home. Could you have controlled your anger and possibly done that?"

"I don't think so, Dad. I was too mad at David for what he did to my sister."

"Will you try the next time someone acts like he just did?"

"I can try, Dad."

"That's my girl," Mike hugged his daughter. "Let's go and tell Mom."

After the girls were tucked in for the night, Marilyn and Michael relaxed on the couch in the quiet of the TV room with a cup of coffee.

"It's been quite a day for you and the girls, my dear," Mike said sympathetically.

Marilyn leaned toward him. "Thanks for sort of taking over when you got home, Michael. By the time you arrived, Ann wasn't the only one who needed a time-out. I needed one from the girls and everything, too."

"Are you OK with the way I handled it?"

"Ann can *so* get under my skin at times," Marilyn confessed. "She is so stubborn."

"Remind you of someone we know?"

"Oh, stop it, Michael. You know what I mean."

"This was a good learning experience for the girls and their parents, too."

"How so, oh wise one?"

Michael moved alongside his wife by now, kissed her neck, and began to unbutton her blouse.

"The girls stood up for one another today. Susan told us of her reaction very clearly. And Ann gave us a rational explanation for her actions. Both of them promised to try to control their tempers in the future. I'd say that was pretty mature of them."

"And, what did we learn today?"

Michael had pushed Marilyn's blouse off her shoulders and was fumbling with the front catch of her bra.

"We learned that our daughters, for all their bickering, have formed a strong bond with one another. Presently, their methods might be a bit crude and too direct, but we know they will look after one another. I think that's great. Our challenge as parents is to teach them to sort of temper such reactions without discouraging that great loyalty and concern they have for each other. What do you think, my dear?"

He had his wife's bra open now and was doing marvelous things with his hands.

Marilyn managed to whisper, "When did you get so smart?"

"Hanging around you, sweetheart."

***

Later, they were lying on the guest room bed, totally out of breath.

"We've been spending a lot of time in here lately," Mike said.

"Are you complaining?" Marilyn asked.

"Not at all," Mike told her, "As long as it's with you in my arms."

"What would you think about moving our bedroom down here?"

Mike smirked, "It would save a lot of midnight trips upstairs, that's for sure."

"Seriously," Marilyn continued, "the girls are getting sort of big for their small bedroom. We could set up twin beds for Ann and Jackie in our room and leave Susan in the smaller one."

"That's fine with me. Are you going to explain to Ann why Susan gets a room to herself?"

"Oh, ya, that." Marilyn realized. "Why is it my job?"

"Because you always think of something."

"Thanks a lot. Why do I always get the tough jobs?"

"Cause you're the mom."

"Oh, ya. How can I forget?"

Mike propped himself on his right elbow. "Want to finish our conversation about the trip to Detroit this summer?"

"Not ready to make love again, big fella?"

"That all depends on whether or not I can get a little help from my partner here."

It was Marilyn's turn to use her hands. She moved toward her husband and used them to explore some. "You mean like that?"

"Oh, ya!"

They didn't talk again for some time.

Marilyn was the one who spoke first.

"I talked with the folks about staying with the kids if we went to Detroit. They'd love to have the kids to themselves for two weeks. Can you take your vacation, then?" she asked.

"Actually, it's an ideal time. With the midterm elections coming up, all of the Congressmen will be home campaigning. There won't be much work around here for staffers like me."

Marilyn added. "Our budget would be strained, though. Will Harold find us a place to stay, free?"

"I'll ask him tomorrow, sweetheart."

"Should be fun," Marilyn said, snuggling up to her husband. "Don't you think?"

"It sure will be a change of pace for us," Mike surmised. "I'll miss the kids, though."

"Me too. But, it should be good for them. Put your arms around me, Michael. I'm getting chilly."

"You mean we're done?"

"Glutton."

PHILADELPHIA

A ten o'clock appointment had been arranged with Arlen Specter in his Philadelphia office.

Burke and Ryan were ushered into a conference room.

"Good morning, gentlemen," Specter said. He stepped forward, extending his hand in greeting to each of his two visitors.

"I'm having a cup of coffee," he said. "Can I get you a cup?"

"Yes, sir," Harold responded. "We left town a bit early and missed our second cup."

"Speak for yourself, Harold," Burke remarked. "I didn't even have my first cup." All three men laughed.

"Cream and sugar, gentlemen?"

"Black will do for us both, Mr. Specter."

"I read that you're a candidate for the circuit court back in Detroit, Mr. Ryan."

"Yes, that's true."

"Well, with a name like Ryan, you should have a leg up on most of the others on the ballot, don't you think?"

"I hope so, Mr. Specter. It's a crowded field. There are probably fifty lawyers who've put their names on the ballot just for the publicity they can gain. So, name recognition is important for voters who are trying to make their selections. I hope the name Ryan jumps out at a whole bunch of them."

"Well, good luck with that," Specter said. "I take it you two are here to question me on the workings of the Warren Commission. Is that correct?"

"Yes, sir," Burke agreed. "We appreciate the time you have taken to see us."

"Not a problem. With all the conspiracy theorists peddling books about the Kennedy assassination, I'm anxious to defend the work of the Warren Commission."

Mike handed Specter a copy of the U.S. News and World Report interview Specter had given in 1966.

Then he explained. "In this interview, most of the questions asked and answered cover our area of interest. Would you like to correct any of your answers before we begin?"

"Not really, gentlemen," Specter told them.

Ryan joined the questioning. "One question not asked during that interview had to do with the Dallas medical personnel. It appears that many of them insisted that the wound to Kennedy's throat was an entry wound. In the interview you gave to Mr. Epstein, you said that the Chief Justice called you into his office on March 15, 1964. You told Epstein that Warren wanted you to go to Dallas and 'clear up the confusion over the bullets.' What confusion was that, sir?" Burke asked.

"There was a conflict between the FBI Report and what was reported in the Dallas press. The former said that three shots were fired from behind the president by one shooter. The Dallas press quoted Parkland ER medical people who said that one round struck the president's throat from the front."

"So this is what you went to Dallas to clear up?"

"Yes, that's right. "

"How did you clear it up, sir?" Ryan continued.

"I spent nine days there, during which time I deposed all the doctors who had seen the wounds."

"Epstein quoted you as saying that 'All (Dallas medical personnel) agreed that there was no basis for concluding the throat wound was an entrance wound.' Was his quote accurate, sir?"

"Essentially, yes," Specter said.

"Translating your lawyer talk for my friend, Burke, sir," Ryan urged, "are you saying that all of the doctors recanted their earlier statements that the president's throat wound was an entry wound?"

"Essentially, yes," Specter insisted.

Burke interrupted. "Sir," he began, "I don't understand why the possibility that the president's throat wound came from the front presented a problem. Could you explain that, sir?"

"I'd be happy to, Mr. Burke," Specter began, "First, the FBI people found three shell casings in the sniper's nest at the Book Depository. They insisted that this confirmed that three shots were fired from that location. They further concluded that all three of those shots were fired by one assassin, and all hit their human targets."

"Secondly," Specter continued, "we read an opinion piece published in a Dallas newspaper that a shot hit the president from the front. This, in addition to the Tague shot, really muddied the water."

"Did Warren fear that it raised a question about the possibility of multiple assassins?"

"Actually, the Chief Justice feared that a debate on this issue would have a very divisive effect on the people of the United States. He wanted it cleared up quickly."

Burke snapped, "It appears, sir, that the Chief Justice wanted to justify the lone assassin conclusion of the FBI Report that had been issued in December."

Specter snapped back, "The Chief Justice was only interested in the truth, Mr. Burke. I know that for a fact."

Burke pushed on, "Are you aware, sir, that last fall, in a Harris-*Washington Post* survey, 67% of the adults in this nation refused to believe the single assassin claim the FBI made?"

"I don't pay much attention to polls, Mr. Burke."

Harold Ryan said, "Another point not addressed in your *U.S. News* interview was the issue about the number of shots fired that day in Dealey Plaza."

"What about it, Mr. Ryan?"

"Without worrying about which shot was fired first or second, etc., can we agree that one shot hit a curb and injured Mr. Tague?"

"Yes, I think so."

"And, can we agree that another shot hit the president's head, the one called the kill shot?"

"All right," Specter agreed, "I think so."

"Another bullet was found during the autopsy at Bethesda Hospital and given to Admiral Burkley, wasn't it?"

"I don't know about that one. If there was, it was never put in as evidence with the Warren Commission. That is entirely possible since the admiral gave it to one of the two FBI agents present at the autopsy. The FBI never informed anyone in my office," Specter complained.

"That could be true, sir," Ryan continued. "But the bullet was found at Bethesda Hospital during the autopsy of President Kennedy. I have a copy of the receipt that FBI agents gave to Admiral Burkley. So, it would seem that our bullet count is now up to three."

"If you say so, Mr. Ryan," Specter said uncomfortably.

"So, did a fourth bullet wound Governor Connally?"

"No, Mr. Ryan," Specter insisted. "A bullet passed through President Kennedy's neck, out his throat, and then into Governor Connally."

"Is that a fourth shot, sir?"

"Only if the bullet you say was found at Bethesda is legitimate. And, you must admit, Mr. Ryan, a chain of evidence was never properly established for that alleged bullet."

Burke spoke up, "Sorta like the pristine bullet mysteriously found on a gurney at Parkland Hospital?"

"Not at all like the bullet found at Parkland, Mr. Burke."

"If you say so, Mr. Specter," Burke responded.

"If you don't mind, sir," Ryan said, "I'd like to return to the subject of the testimony given you by the medical personnel at Parkland Hospital. I must tell you that I had a very different response during my interviews last month from the same medical people you interviewed there back in March 1964. They all still insist that the president's throat wound was one of entry. And, they all insist that they told you that during your interrogation of them in March of 1964."

"As a trial attorney, Mr. Ryan," Specter reminded him. "you know very well that time erodes the memory of witnesses. Eighteen months ago, they told me the throat wound could possibly have been an exit wound. Last week, they told you it was not. Such a change in the recollection of an event happens to witnesses all the time. It happens for a whole bunch of reasons having nothing to do with the truth. You know that, Mr. Ryan."

Ryan responded. "I must admit time can change what a witness remembers. But, I submit, sir, that it would be hard to find such a large number of highly trained witnesses all forgetting the details of such a traumatic event."

"Sir," Mike Burke asked, "I've read your description of the wounding of both the president and Governor Connally. The Commission decided that one bullet entered the back of President Kennedy's neck, exited his throat, then wounded the governor. Do I have that correct?"

"Yes, you do. Please look at this drawing with wound sites marked by Dr.Humes during the Bethesda Hospital autopsy. He said that the back wound entered the president at an angle of 45 to 60 degrees."

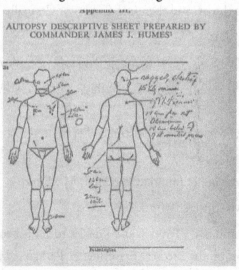

At this point, Ryan interrupted and said, "By the way, Mr. Specter, Admiral Burkley, who was in attendance at both the Parkland ER and at the Bethesda Hospital autopsy, verified what Dr. Humes drew on what pathologists call a face sheet, like this one."

"Now, sir," Burke resumed questioning Mr. Specter, "please look at this autopsy photograph of President Kennedy's back. You can see a wound to the right of the spine and about five inches from the neck. It is marked with an x. Can you see that, sir?"

"If this is truly a photograph of President Kennedy, yes, I can see the mark."

Ryan interrupted again, "Both Dr. Humes and Admiral Burkley verified this as the only wound they saw on the president's back. And Dr. Thornton Boswell, a pathologist who assisted Dr. Humes, told me that this wound was only a few inches deep and had no exit path in President Kennedy's body."

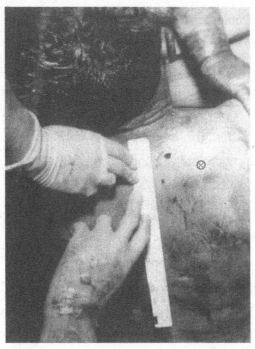

"None of these three doctors reported seeing another wound at the back of the neck."

Then, Burke asked, "So, how did a bullet that entered the president from be-hind at a sharp downward angle several inches below the neck come out five or so inches higher at the base of his throat where the knot of a necktie would be?"

"I'm not an anatomy expert, gentlemen," Specter said lightly. "Nor was I during my work with the Commission. Dr. Humes suggested to me the possibility that a bullet had exited the president through his neck, causing the wound he saw at the front of JFK's throat. You'll really have to talk with him about this particular issue."

Burke leaned forward. "Are you saying, sir, that you based the 'single bullet theory' on the offhand suggestion of a Navy doctor?"

"Talk to Dr. Humes, Mr. Burke," Specter repeated.

"Also, sir," Burke asked. "The Commission narrative said the back wound was at the base of the neck. How did this wound move up several inches?"

"You can ask Congressman Ford that question, Mr. Burke. He was in charge of editing the final version of the Commission's Report." Specter said.

"Mr. Epstein also reported that you said you gave the members of the Commission a choice; accept the 'single bullet theory' or begin looking for a second assassin. Is that what you said, Mr. Specter?" Ryan asked.

"Yes, it was."

"Why didn't the members of the Commission see the autopsy photographs?" Burke asked.

"The members didn't see them because Chief Justice Warren had them locked away in the National Achieves as sealed evidence."

"But, weren't they evidence important to the Commission?"

"Despite that, Chairman Warren had them locked away," Specter revealed. "The story goes that Robert Kennedy talked to the Chief Justice and expressed his concern that the photographs might fall into the hands of unscrupulous tabloids. To avoid causing the Kennedy family additional pain, he had them sealed."

"How was it decided to set September 28, 1964, as a deadline for the Commission's report?"

"I believe it was Congressman Ford who said that date was chosen so that everything would be finished before the fall elections. In actual fact, though, Chairman Warren set the date. You'll have to ask him why he did that," Specter answered. "I do know, though, that the press was full of unfounded rumors. He felt it was important that the people of our country have definitive answers as quickly as possible."

WASHINGTON D.C.

Burke and Ryan were meeting in their conference room with Marilyn and a stenographer.

"Do you need to conduct any more interviews?" Marilyn asked.

"I don't think so," Ryan answered. "I think we have all we need to prove our point."

"The point being?" she asked.

"That there was more than one assassin in Dealey Plaza on November 22, 1963," Ryan answered.

"So, Harold," Mike asked. "How do you think we should present to Chairman Conyers and Minority Leader Ford our study and our conclusion?"

"I would suggest that we write up a cover sheet stating our charge. Then we attach the evidence we uncovered and state our conclusion."

"That sounds pretty straightforward, as far as it goes," Mike added.

"What more should we do, Mike?"

"I think we need to also develop a recommendation page to follow the ones you mentioned."

Marilyn spoke up at this point. "How about this? We start with a section outlining the charge you two were given. Then, we follow that with a findings page. The third section will list references that support the finding. The last section would be a recommendation page."

"Sounds good," Harold agreed, "Let's separate for one hour and write this thing up. Marilyn, you've explained what we are about to enough people while getting us appointments. So you take the section stating the charge we were given by the Judiciary Committee. I'll write up the section dealing with the evidence given me by the medical people."

Mike suggested, "I'll take the non-medical witnesses, the re-enactors, and the information I was given by the two survey men. Then let's put those three together before we write up the conclusion and the recommendation sections. That'll work, won't it?"

"Seems like it should," Harold agreed, "Meet you two back here at this table in one hour."

***

Back at the table, Marilyn began. "I think it would be helpful if I shared my thoughts about your charge before we get into your sections."

"Fine, what have you got?" Mike asked.

Marilyn handed a sheet of paper to Harold and another one to Mike. On each, she had typed several short paragraphs followed by a question and the following explanation.

***

Page One: Title Page: The Burke – Ryan Report

Page Two: The charge of the Judiciary Committee.

In a 1966 Harris-Washington Post poll, sixty-seven percent of Americans said they did not believe the single shooter conclusion announced in the FBI Report of December 1963 and the Warren Commission Report of September 1964.

In reaction, members of the House Judiciary Committee directed their chairman, Congressman John Conyers, and their minority leader, Congressman Gerald Ford, to initiate a study of the evidence surrounding the assassination of President John F. Kennedy.

The question the committee wished answered first was:

Did Oswald act alone?

"To arrive at the answer to this one question, investigators talked with persons involved in the post-assassination investigations and looked at other bodies of evidence collected for the FBI and Warren reports.

The Burke – Ryan Report, done for the Judiciary Committee, deals with:

Directionality: Did all the shots come from behind as claimed?

Shots: How many shots were fired? Were more than three shots fired?

Shooters: Were all the shots fired by one assassin? Was there more than one assassin?

This report will devote one section to each of the above questions. An appendix and notes dealing with the testimony taken will follow.

This will be followed by another section presenting findings and possible recommendations.'

***

"Well, guys," Marilyn asked, "Does this give you a clear and acceptable layout for your report?"

"I believe it does, Marilyn," Mike decided. "What do you think, Harold?"

"Let's use it to complete our report. As we go, we can always make adjustments. Why don't you sort of referee, Marilyn, as Mike and I insert names and citations in each section?"

"I can do that," Marilyn agreed, "Before we start, though, let me get our stenographer, Betty, in here. She can do her magic faster than any of us can write."

During the next few hours, they cut and pasted together a rough draft of their report.

"What do you think, Harold?" Mike asked. "Were our findings soundly supported?"

"Yes. I believe reasonable people would think we did make our case, Mike," Harold responded. "I know I feel comfortable putting my name on this report.

"It helped that the editors at *Life Magazine* recommended another look be taken at the 1964 Warren Commission's findings."

***

Over the next two days, Betty was kept busy typing fresh versions for the three of them to edit.

"I believe we've just about polished this report to death, guys," Marilyn decided. "Enough is enough; you've got to stop sometime."

"I say we go with this version, Harold," Mike said. "Agreed?"

"Yup," he responded. "You OK with that, Marilyn?"

"You bet," she said. "I've had enough. Let's go with this."

Harold turned to Betty. "You will be pleased to know, young lady, that we are finished."

"Thank the Lord," she responded. "I've been seeing these pages in my sleep lately. How many copies are you going to need?"

"We'll need three copies for us, one for Congressman Conyers, another for Congressman Ford, and one for the file; six in all."

"When will you need them?"

"Today is Wednesday," Mike noted. "Can you have them delivered to everyone Friday afternoon?

"I think so, Mr. Burke," Betty promised. "Can you pick your copies up Friday any time after three?"

Mike turned to Harold. "Does that give you time to catch your flight for Detroit?"

"I think so," he figured. "I'll be in your office at three sharp, Betty. If I can pick up my copy then I'll be able to make my flight."

"See you Friday at three, Betty," Mike said. "What are you gonna' do until the weekend, Harold?"

"I'm going to hang around the office here the rest of today and tomorrow, Mike," Harold announced. "I can use the government's nickel to check in with people back in Detroit by phone. Then, I'll be back in D.C. Monday evening.

"Give me a call when you get back, Harold. Maybe we can meet at my house Tuesday to go over our Wednesday presentation to Conyers and Ford."

"That might work; I'll check in with you Monday evening then, Mike."

SILVER SPRING

The girls were in the basement playing school. As Marilyn had predicted, Ann had become the teacher. Her subject this Saturday morning was the proper way to dress a Barbie doll for a date with Ken.

Even though she was now the pupil, the eldest of the Burke children was not going quietly.

"What kind of date is this, teacher?" she asked.

"What difference does that make?"

"A lot," Susan shot back, "Are they going to the beach or out to eat and a movie. Is Barbie going to wear a bathing suit or jeans?"

"I think jeans would work." Ann decided.

Jackie asked, "Will Mom wear jeans tonight when she and Dad go out?"

"What has that got to do with Barbie's date, anyways?" Ann snapped.

"I don't know," Jackie mumbled, "I just wondered. Where are they going?"

Susan answered. "I think they're going to that Chinese restaurant they like and maybe a movie."

"Yuk! How can they like Chinese food?" Jackie grimaced.

"I know," Susan agreed, "There are a lot of things older people do that are sorta weird."

"Now, students!" Ann shouted, fearing she was losing her class, "Finish dressing Barbie for her date. Remember, Dad is going to take us to McDonald's for lunch when we finish our class."

"Hooray!" Susan and Jackie shouted.

***

Upstairs, the Burkes were discussing their trip to Michigan. Money was the current issue.

"I've gone over our budget, Michael," Marilyn began, "And we have enough to cover all our Maryland expenses while we are gone. The pinch comes with finding funds for the potential Michigan expenses."

"I've talked to Harold about this," Mike responded. "He has arranged lodging for us and $300 in expense money. That should handle food and auto expenses while we're in Detroit. But, I worry about our travel expenses on the road going and returning."

"How much do you figure that will cost?"

"Gasoline alone could cost us around $100. If we take a cooler with sandwiches and snacks, that will save us stopping to eat. And if we drive straight through, we would save on motel costs. So, I figure we need around $150 round trip tops in travel costs. Can we manage that?"

"You know that cookie jar in the kitchen?"

"Oh, ya," Mike said, "The one with no cookies in it."

"Well, smart ass, why don't you get it down off the fridge." Marilyn teased. "Let's see what's in it."

Mike walked back into the TV room with the jar. "What the hell! It's full of loose change and a few bills."

"Now you know what happens to the loose change you put on the dresser every night. Let's count it," his wife chuckled.

He dumped the contents, and the two of them sat on the floor and began to sort out the change and bills.

"Well, I'll be darned," Mike exclaimed," You little dickens. You've got $62 squirreled away in this jar."

"And, we've got a couple of hundred in the savings account," Marilyn reminded him, "So if we're careful, we should be all right on the road."

"What about the two flat tires last month? You had ours repaired, not replaced. That could be a problem on the road, ya' know."

"Let's put $100 in the glove compartment as sort of a tire fund. Just in case, all right?" Marilyn suggested.

"Sounds good," Mike agreed, "Have you told the kids about the trip?"

"Let's do it tomorrow after their naps."

"That's as good a time as any. But, right now, it's off to McDonald's." Mike went to the top of the basement stairs.

"Are you ready, girls?" he shouted.

"Hooray," they hollered in response and ran up the stairs.

***

After their naps that afternoon, Mike and the girls were walking back from the park. They had made the rounds of the swings, merry-go-round, the slide, and the teeter-totter. They had had a good time. But supper was waiting; their favorite, mac and cheese.

As usual, Mr. Joe was sitting on his front porch watching the neighborhood while he smoked his cigarette.

"Hi, Mr. Joe," Susan greeted with a smile. "How are you today?"

"I'm fine, Susie," he responded, "Have a good time at the park?"

"Yes, we did," Jackie responded.

"Hi, Annie," Joe greeted with a chuckle.

Ann looked directly at him but said nothing. Then she turned her head and walked past his porch and down the driveway toward the back door of the Burke home.

Mike noticed. "Annie," he asked, "Didn't you hear Mr. Joe say hello to you?"

"Yes, I did. But I'm still mad at him, Dad." She said.

"Hold on, young lady. Mr. Joe spoke to you very nicely. It was rude not to return his greeting. So, right now you are going to go back and answer him. "

"Oh, Dad. Do I have to?"

"Yes, you do. And you will do it with a smile on your face."

Mike waited and watched as Ann walked back down the driveway to his neighbor's porch.

"Hello, Mr. Joe," he heard her say.

"Well, hello, Annie," Joe responded. "Did you and your sisters have a good time at the park?"

"Yes, we did, thank you," she answered, "Good night, Mr. Joe. I have to go in for dinner."

"Good night, Annie."

As she walked by her father, he said.

"Now wasn't that better?"

"I'm still mad at him, Dad."

Mike laughed out loud.

Oh, my goodness! I'm glad she's not mad at me.

***

The Burkes were at their favorite Chinese restaurant savoring their hot soup. As usual, Mike had ordered almond chicken with white rice and an egg roll.

Marilyn sipped her egg-drop soup and waited for her entree and brown rice to be served. As usual, she ordered a dish Mike didn't recognize and called something he could not pronounce. Meanwhile, he savored his won-ton soup and fried noodles.

Marilyn paused, "Now that you have had a chance to think about it, do you want to change anything in the report?"

"Can't think of a thing," he responded, "how about you?"

"I read it over when you and the girls were at the park. Quite frankly, I think it's fine the way it is."

"I hope Harold's opinion that we made our case that Oswald did not act alone holds up before the committee."

"Don't you expect Congressman Ford to react negatively?" Marilyn asked, "After all, you guys sure stuck it to him."

"Yes, we did. But we had little choice. He's the member of the Commission who led the charge to support the FBI Report. And he was the only member of the Commission who made extended public statements that were printed in *Life Magazine*. He also claimed that the Commission had decided on a lone gunman who fired just three shots from the rear of the motorcade. And Ford insists in his statements and writing that this conclusion was reached only after a thorough examination of all the testimony and reenactments. In one *Life Magazine* article, he even states that there was no credible evidence of any shots fired from in front of the president. The actual evidence he insists the Commission examined clearly refutes his statements and articles to the contrary. He made himself the poster boy of the Warren Commission. So, we had no choice but to put the spotlight on him."

"Do you think he'll want to bury your report, Michael?"

"I suppose he will."

"So, what will you and Harold do about that?" Marilyn asked.

"You and I are going to get together with him next Tuesday. You can ask him then."

"I'm asking you now, Michael," Marilyn pressed, "What are you inclined to do if Conyers and Ford do nothing with your report?"

"Remember, sweetheart. Harold goes back to Detroit and his cushy new job. I have to stay here and work for these guys. What do you think I should do?"

"You know what I think, Michael," Marilyn snapped in a whisper, "I think you should stick it to these bastards and release your report to someone in the press."

Mike said softly, "We'll meet with Harold and discuss this. Who knows, maybe Conyers and Ford will accept our recommendation and get behind a new investigation?"

On the verge of real anger, Marilyn responded. "That will be a cold day in hell, Michael. And, you know it."

"Please, Marilyn," Mike begged. "Let's change the subject and enjoy our evening out, OK?"

"All right, Michael. Let's change the subject," she said mischievously, "How about those Baltimore Orioles? They've won ten of their last twelve games."

Mike laughed and almost choked on his soup.

What a woman!

Their food arrived, and they did enjoy the rest of their evening out.

While Mike walked the neighborhood babysitter to her nearby house, Marilyn checked on the girls and prepared for Mike's return.

When he did, he walked into the living room to see candles lit and Marilyn in her shorty nightgown, lounging on the couch with a drink in her hand.

"The night's not over yet, Michael," she told him dreamily, "Your drink is on the coffee table."

He picked up the small glass and sipped. "Ummm, what's this? Tia Maria, my favorite after-dinner drink. You're full of surprises, my dear."

"I've got another one for you if you join me on the couch."

"I thought you preferred the guest bed."

"Who said anything about bed, big guy?"

Mike sat on the couch, and Marilyn put her bare feet on his lap.

"How about giving me a nice foot rub?"

"Is that my surprise?" he asked.

"Not hardly," she whispered, "The surprise comes after."

WASHINGTON D.C.

They didn't meet at the Burke home because, as Harold pointed out,

"What if we decide on some changes? We'll need Betty. So, better we meet in our D.C. office."

After greetings and coffee poured, the three of them settled back.

"Have any changes in mind, Harold?" Marilyn asked.

"Not a one at this moment," he said, "I think it's fine just the way it is. You, Mike?"

"Not a one at this moment," Mike responded with a big grin.

All three of them burst into laughter.

"Good thing Uncle Sam is paying for my babysitter today, Harold. Otherwise, I'd have a bone to pick with you," Marilyn informed him, "Now, what do we do?"

"I suggest we talk about the future of the Burke family, Marilyn," Harold said.

"Do you know what he's talking about, Michael?"

"Not a clue," Mike assured his wife, "What's up, Harold?"

"Before I answer, let's take a walk just in case these walls have ears."

At a nearby park, they settled into some seats.

"This past weekend wasn't all campaigning," Harold began, "I also got my people and the union folks to agree to let me select my own court clerk after I'm elected. I want you to accept that position, Mike."

In the silence that followed, Harold just sat there and smiled. Finally, he added, "Marilyn, I thought you wanted Mike to get out of Washington and away from those people you called 'bastards.'"

"I suppose I did. But, I didn't count on such a long commute for Michael to get to his job every day."

"I suppose that would be a problem," Harold agreed, laughing, "But it wouldn't be all that difficult from the house you'd have in Detroit."

"Just like that, Harold," Mike finally spoke up. "Just like that, we're supposed to pick up and leave Maryland?"

"You two don't have to answer me right now. Spend your two weeks with me in Detroit. Get a feel for the place and the people. Look over the schools and the housing. We'll talk again. Remember, I have to win the damn election before there is a job for either of us. Let's get back to the office and prepare for tomorrow."

Back at the office, Harold sort of led the discussion.

"As a staffer, you must know, Mike, that committee members seldom read all the documents you prepare for them. So, first, we should assume that neither Conyers nor Ford will have read our report beforehand. With that in mind, we must walk them through it and thereby lead them to the conclusion we've already reached."

"That's not much different than the prep work I do with committee members before open sessions, Harold," Mike said.

"Exactly my point. So, why don't I start out with page 2 and page 3?" Harold suggested, "You can pick up the next section at that point."

"Fine," Mike responded, "I'll take pages 4, 5, and 7. You pick up page 8, 'Were all the shots fired by one assassin?'"

"That's good," Harold said. "Then, I'll walk them through Appendix A and B. You can do Appendix C, D, and E."

Burke concluded, "And, I suggest you take them through our 'Findings and Recommendation."

"It seems like we have our homework for tonight, Mike."

"Right. See you here tomorrow morning, Harold. The first one of us in makes the coffee."

"Got it."

WASHINGTON D.C.

Burke and Ryan were shown into Congressman Conyers' private conference room. Congressman Ford was already seated.

Conyers rose and shook each man's hand.

"Welcome, gentlemen," he greeted, "You know Gerry Ford, I'm sure, don't you, Harold?"

"I certainly do, John," Ryan assured him, "Good morning, Congressman. Good to see you again."

"It certainly is, Harold," Ford responded, "I hope that little episode in Dallas last month didn't cause you any problems."

"Luckily, the shooter missed. But, the FBI auto he hit wasn't as fortunate." All the men laughed a bit at that comment.

Conyers began the meeting.

"You know Betty, gentlemen," Conyers began, "As you recall, she worked with you on the preparation of your report. I have asked her to take notes of our meeting. I hope you don't mind."

"Certainly not, sir," Burke answered.

"You two have been busy, it appears. You have done a rather complete job in your effort to prove or disprove your central question. Do either of you have any comments to make before either Congressman Ford or I get into the particulars?"

"Yes, sir, I do," Harold Ryan said.

"Go ahead, Harold," Conyers invited.

"Mike and I realized from the start that we could not examine all the interviews and all the data gathered by the FBI for its December 1963 Report. We certainly were not staffed to review in detail the twenty-some volumes of the Warren Commission Report either. So, we focused on answering one question, 'Did Oswald act alone'? To answer that central question, we personally interviewed witnesses key to each element of the study. As you can see on page 2 of the report, we looked at three elements:

Directionality: did all the shots come from behind?

Shots: how many shots were fired?

Shooters: were all the shots fired by one assassin?"

"Gentlemen," Mike began, "The first of these elements, 'directionality,' demands we look at the possibility that one or more shots came from the area of the Grassy Knoll. The Warren Commission interviewed or looked at the testimony taken by the FBI of thirty-eight witnesses. All of them reported that one or more shots came from the Grassy Knoll or saw suspicious activity in that area. So, I personally interviewed the most credible of those thirty-eight. Mr. O'Donnell, cited here, was not interviewed. If you will please turn to page 6, 'How many shots were fired?' Here we have listed all the verified shots fired that day in Dealey Plaza. These do not include all the confusing claims of bullet fragments found in the vehicle, on the street, and in the grass. Simple arithmetic should lead most anyone to see that both the FBI Report and the Warren Commission were mistaken in their conclusions on this matter; more than three shots were fired on November 22, 1963, in Daeley Plaza."

"Please turn to page ten, gentlemen," Harold continued. "I interviewed medical personnel at Parkland Memorial Hospital. All of these witnesses were interviewed by Warren Commission lawyers in the spring of 1964. I compared the testimony they gave then to that given to me, and it had not changed in any way. They still insist that the president's throat wound was one of entry, not exit. Other physicians who were present in the emergency room working to save President Kennedy's life testified about the head wound he suffered. All of them insisted that the head wound they saw in the emergency room was an exit wound. Other credible witnesses included three Secret Service agents in the motorcade, one motorcycle policeman following the president's car, and the nurse who prepared his body for transport to Washington. All of them testified to a massive wound on the back of the head, not an entry wound."

Then, Burke directed the two Congressmen to Appendix D. "In this section, you will notice some representations from witnesses you might have noticed on previous pages. If we were to address the question, 'Were all the shots fired by one assassin?' It was necessary to direct the reader of this report to those who testified on the throat wound, directionality, and the Grassy Knoll sections. And while the following may seem redundant, may I direct you to Appendix E. In this section, we quote the two men who directed firing tests using the rifle attributed to Oswald. In the testimony of the weapons specialist FBI Special Agent Robert Frazier to the Warren Commission, he said his best time firing three rounds and hitting a stationary target 100 yards away was 4.6 seconds. But he also testified under oath that he would have to add a second per round if he was firing at a moving target, for a total of 6.6 seconds. Nevertheless, the Commission used the faster speed of 4.6 seconds and said Oswald hit his moving targets three times within that time span. Ronald Simmons, Chief of the Infantry Weapons Evaluation Branch of the Ballistics Research Laboratory of the Department of the Army, recruited three expert riflemen. They fired 21 shots at a stationary target. Only one of his experts hit the target within the Warren Commission's time limit of 5.15 seconds. Both of these reports were buried in the Warren Commission Report and ignored when the commissioners decided that one man hit all his targets three times within 4.3 seconds on November 22, 1963."

Harold Ryan didn't give the two Congressmen time to react. "Gentlemen, please turn to page 22 titled 'Findings.' You will note on this page that we took the liberty of stating the three findings our research led us to believe. There was more than one shooter who participated in the assassination of President Kennedy. More than three shots were fired in the assassination plot to kill President Kennedy. There were shots fired at President Kennedy from in front of the motorcade as well as from behind. "We have followed that with a single recommendation:

"One conclusion is inescapable: the national interest deserves a clear resolution of the doubts. A new investigating body should be set up, perhaps at the initiative of Congress. In a scrupulously objective and unhurried atmosphere, without the pressure to assure a shocked country, it should re-examine the evidence and consider other evidence the Warren Commission failed to evaluate. *Life Magazine: Editorial of November 25, 1966. Page 49b.* Because this clearly states the obvious, we took the liberty of borrowing this recommendation from a rather recent *Life Magazine* editorial from the date stated above."

"Do you have any questions of either of us, gentlemen?" Harold concluded.

"I have a question, Ryan," Congressman Ford said.

Ford did not use my former title, Congressman. He's too schooled in the protocol not to have omitted that courtesy on purpose.

"Yes, Ford," Harold shot back. "How can I help you?"

Ford's face colored a bit. "Using my quotes as you did makes it appear that I had more influence on the formation of the Commission's final report than was the case."

Burke replied. "But, sir," he said. "You were the only member of the Commission who chose to be front and center with an article in *Life Magazine* of October 2, 1964." Mike put a copy of that issue on the table in front of Congressman Ford. If you are suggesting that you did not write the sentence we quoted or that we took it out of context, we will be happy to correct that right now, sir."

After a brief pause, Ford said. "That will not be necessary, gentlemen."

"I have a question of you, Ford," Harold said.

Ford visibly bristled at the obvious omission of his title.

"What would that be, Ryan?"

"In a *Life Magazine* article, you assured the American people that, and I quote, … 'No one at the time saw anything suspicious.'"

"What about it, Ryan?"

"Thirty-eight people interviewed by the FBI or your investigators said otherwise. Credible witnesses standing on or near the Grassy Knoll swore that they heard one or more shots from behind them or by the fence area, or they saw something unusual or were prevented from investigating by men showing false Secret Service identification. Given this evidence at your disposal, how could you tell the nation, 'There is no evidence of a second man, or other shots, of other guns.'?"

Agitated, Ford leaned into the table toward Ryan.

"My colleagues on the Commission depended upon the integrity of both the information supplied by the FBI and our investigators. And in addition, we were under a very tight deadline to issue our report. You have the advantage of over two years of data gathering, Ryan." he insisted.

"If you say so, Congressman Ford," Ryan concluded.

Burke asked Congressman Conyers. "Do you have any questions, sir?"

"I don't think so, Mike," he replied, "I'm just happy I didn't write an article in support of the Warren Commission Report." Only Burke laughed at his boss's light-hearted reply.

"Would you like me to supply a copy of this report to each member of the Judiciary Committee, sir?" Burke asked.

"Not right now, Mike," Conyers replied, "I understand you're taking two weeks off. When you return will be soon enough to discuss releasing this report. I'll talk to you about it then.

"Let me take this opportunity to thank you, Congressman Ryan, for the time you took away from your campaign for Wayne County Circuit Judge back in Detroit. Your effort is appreciated.

"Thank you, sir," Ryan said. "And allow me to thank you for the support given our investigation by your staff."

The men stood and shook hands.

On the way out, Conyers cornered Harold.

"Harold, with Congress adjourned until the fall, I'll be back in Detroit next week for a while. Be sure to contact my staff there if you think I can be of any help in your campaign."

"Thank you, John," Harold said. "It's kind of you to offer. Believe me, I can use your help. So, I'll be in touch."

***

Back in Conyer's office, Congressman Ford, the Minority Leader of the Judiciary Committee, said, "I want this piece of crap buried, John."

"Sure you do, Gerry," Conyers replied, suppressing a chuckle at his Republican colleague's discomfort. "But, a majority of our committee members asked for this investigation. Remember? So, I'll need you to tell me how you will manage to deep-six this report, OK?"

"Anyway, I don't want it released now," Ford insisted. "It makes me look like I participated in a cover-up. It makes fools of the Warren Commission."

"Gerry, the best I can do is to hold on to this until after the fall elections. But you had better think of some reason not to release this after that. I'm not going to stiff my members just to save you some embarrassment."

"Work with me on this, John."

"I will, Gerry," Conyers assured Ford." So, if the contents of this report get out, it will not be from me. But I suggest that you not share it with your friends over at the Bureau right now. They almost made a mess of things in Dallas and at Burke's home. I don't think we can trust them. Do you?"

Ford ignored the dig at Hoover and the FBI.

"What about Ryan and Burke?" Ford asked.

"Come on, Gerry," Conyers said. "Just calm down. Ryan is running for elective office, where he needs support from the UAW and the AFL-CIO. It's not in his interests right now to get them angry with him by releasing this. He knew you were intentionally rude to him at our meeting, but he'll not upset things. I guarantee you that his election is foremost in his mind right now. As far as Burke is concerned, he's my man. I'll take care of him.

THE ARMY-NAVY CLUB

Mike, Harold, and Marilyn were having lunch at the Army-Navy Club. Harold had been rooming there during his work in Washington. He was planning to leave for Detroit first thing in the morning.

"Tell me everything," Marilyn urged them.

"You first, Harold," Mike suggested. "You're the one who really took Ford on."

"Oh, good!" Marilyn exclaimed, "Was there blood on the floor when you finished, Harold?"

"Not really, Marilyn," he responded with a chuckle, "But once he started being rude to me, I let him have it. He whined some because we used two quotes from his *Life Magazine* article back in 1964 to suggest a Warren Commission cover-up. Ford really bristled at that. When he gave us some bull-shit excuse for ignoring all kinds of evidence, I asked him point blank how he could deceive the American public in the face of such overwhelming evidence. He was not a happy person when we finished."

Mike raised his water glass. "You really roasted his ass, Harold. I must say. So, I offer a toast; to the three musketeers."

"Hear, hear," Harold and Marilyn said in unison.

"What do you think they'll do with your report?" Marilyn asked.

Harold spoke first. "Based on my past experience in D.C., Ford will want to bury and forget it. But Conyers won't care if it gets out. After all, Ford is a Republican. It wouldn't hurt Conyers at all to see Ford embarrassed. He just wouldn't want his fingerprints on the release."

"I agree, Marilyn," Mike added, "The two men have to work together because of their positions on the Judiciary Committee. So, their public face is friendly. But they don't go out for drinks together, and their wives don't travel in the same social circle. Conyers wouldn't want to be seen doing anything too public to hurt Ford."

"How about you two?" Marilyn asked, "Will either of you release the report?"

Mike spoke first this time. "I'd like to give Conyers time to figure out a way to release it. Besides, if I had anything to do with it, my job as a staffer anywhere in Washington would be over."

"I've got an election to worry about," Harold added, "I have no intention of jeopardizing my chances by releasing our report before the November voting."

"So, it would seem that it's in our mutual interest to wait until after the fall election," Marilyn said.

"We must wait at least that long," Harold said firmly.

***

"Now, my friends," Harold changed the subject, "Will you be in Detroit next week?"

Marilyn answered. "My folks are arriving tomorrow, Harold, and we plan to get on the road Saturday morning early. We're going to drive straight through, so I figure we'll be in Detroit late Saturday evening sometime."

"Good to know. I'll have the house on Wayburn Street ready for you. Just call me when you get close, and I'll guide you in."

Harold handed Mike a packet. "The address is 6654 Wayburn. Actually, if you use this AAA travel packet, you could drive right there. It's just off the eastbound Detroit expressway."

"We'll call you just the same, Harold," Mike said.

"Good. My home number is in the packet, too. So, that's it." Harold said, "I'm really looking forward to having you in Detroit and on board the campaign."

He gave Marilyn a hug and shook Mike's hand.

"See you Saturday, Harold."

SILVER SPRING

It was 8 o'clock, and Mike was upstairs, tucking in the kids. It was still light outside, and they could hear the Miles boys playing in front of their house.

The girls were sitting on the bed with Mike.

"Dad," Susan began, "Tell us again why we have to go to bed this early. The streetlights aren't even on, and school is out for the summer."

"You guys need your sleep if you are to grow up healthy and strong. That's why."

Susan fell back on the bed. "Oh, my goodness, Dad. You told us that last summer, too."

"Well, girls, it's still true."

"Why is 8 o'clock the magic number?" Ann asked. "Are you saying that the Miles parents don't care if their boys grow up healthy?"

"No, I'm not saying that. I'm only responsible for how you grow up."

"How old do we have to be before we can stay up later, like to 8:30 or 9 o'clock?" Ann asked.

Mike was beginning to feel the girls were ganging up on him over this issue.

"How about this, girls?" Mike began. "While Mom and I are in Detroit, we'll talk about this. When we return, we will all have a discussion about bedtime. How about that?"

"How about this, Dad," Susan suggested. "When Gramma and Grampa tell you that we were wonderful and everything, we get to stay up until 9 o'clock until school starts. After that, 8:30 will be our bedtime on school nights."

"I think that's a fine idea, Sue," Ann agreed. "I'll even be nice to Mr. Joe while you and Mom are gone. How about that, Dad?"

"Whoa, girls," Mike cautioned. "Mom has a say in this, too. Besides, I'm not comfortable bargaining for good behavior. In fact, I expect you girls will act properly while your grandparents are here. What I will do is talk to Mom on our way to Michigan. Then we'll all talk about this when we get back in two weeks. How do you feel about that, girls?"

"OK, Dad," Susan agreed. "Is that all right with you, Ann?" she asked her sister.

"It's fine with me, Sue," she said, "We'll all decide when Mom and Dad get back. Right, Dad?"

"That's right, girls."

I bet those two planned this whole thing. Good for them. They're working together for a common goal. Now, my job is to get Marilyn to agree to loosening up the bedtime. I wonder if these girls figured that out, too.

***

Mike joined his wife in the front bedroom. She was packing things into suitcases and boxes on the bed.

He got his summer suit, some dress shirts, and his raincoat out of the guest room closet. While he did this, he explained the girls' proposal.

"Why those two little sneaks!" she exclaimed. "You know why they asked you first and not me?"

"No," Mike said," Tell me why they brought it up to me first and not you."

"Because they know they can wrap you around their little fingers and get their way. They know I would turn them down flat; that's why."

"Why would you turn them down flat, Marilyn?"

"Because."

"Because, why?"

"Because Michael, it is not their role to dictate such things to their parents. That's why," Marilyn said somewhat hotly.

"They weren't dictating anything. They were testing the waters, so to speak. Tell me then, at what stage in their lives do we allow them to have a role in deciding such things, Marilyn?"

"Look, Michael, you dump this thing on me as though I've not got a thing in the world to worry about. But, right now, I've got a million things on my mind, getting ready for our trip," she complained, "Right now, I'm trying to get us packed. Can't we talk about it while we're driving to Michigan?" she suggested. "We'll have plenty of time then."

"That's fine with me," Mike responded. "That's exactly what I told the kids, too. But, I did promise them that we would all sit down and talk about their suggestion when we return."

"That's what I mean," Marilyn chuckled, still folding clothes for their suitcases, "They've got you bamboozled."

"Not at all," Mike protested. "They got my attention on an issue that is important to them, and they made a proposal for us to talk about. That's not bamboozling a parent. Quite the contrary," he continued, "I think they chose a responsible way to approach a topic of mutual interest. They're maturing, sweetheart. I want them to know we're willing to listen to their ideas and to seriously consider them."

"All right, Michael," Marilyn conceded, "We'll try your way. Now hand me that stack of underwear on top of the dresser. I've got to finish packing. My parents will be here tomorrow and will need this room. If I know my father, he'll get up at the crack of dawn and be here for breakfast."

They were, too.

DETROIT

Mike and Marilyn were on the expressway headed north out of Maryland early Saturday morning. This was the first time both of them had been separated from their children. So leaving had been hard.

Traveling at about 65 MPH, they stayed away from the outside lane, leaving that for faster vehicles. Instead, they drove on the inside lane and took it easy in their late-model sedan with its repaired tires. Most of the traffic they experienced passed them like they were standing still.

Even so, they reached the Ohio Turnpike early in the afternoon and realized they would probably be at the Michigan border early in the evening. So, the next time they stopped to use a restroom, Mike called Harold to tell him they would be in Detroit earlier than expected.

"If you're just outside of Toledo, Ohio, I would guess that you should be here by 8 o'clock tonight, Mike," Harold told him.

"As you drive east on the Detroit Expressway, look for the Chandler Park/Outer Drive exit. Stay on the service drive until you get to Wayburn Street, turn right, and come south to 5564. My wife Lillian and I will meet you there."

"Sounds simple enough, Harold," Mike told him, "We have your travel maps, so it shouldn't be a problem. See you then."

Sure enough, the Burkes arrived safe and sound.

Harold introduced them to his wife, and she showed Marilyn the house while the men carried in the luggage.

"This is so nice of you, Lillian, Marilyn said, "Oh, my goodness. You even stocked the fridge."

"Just a few things to get you started," Lillian said, "I'll take you to the A & P down the street tomorrow after church."

"What time is church, by the way?" Marilyn asked.

"We'll pick you up at 9:30 so we can make 10 o'clock Mass at St. John Birchman's. Afterward, we'll have some breakfast and then shop. Does that sound all right to you?"

"Oh, you don't have to go to all that trouble, really," Marilyn assured Lillian.

"No trouble at all," she responded. "Harold and I always go to the 10 o'clock at one church or another. St. Johns is just down the street. We eat out every Sunday, too. So it's a treat for us to have company."

The next day, over breakfast, Harold gave the Burkes a glimpse of what their daily schedule would be like. Marilyn would work in the campaign office, which would be open at 10 a.m. and would close most days twelve hours later. She will work with Alberta Sullivan to fill Ryan's day and evening with appearances and speaking engagements.

Gonzalee Sullivan drove Harold and Lillian to church club meetings, neighborhood clubs, coffee hour gatherings, as well as political meetings in the evening. Mike went with them to pass out literature and to become familiar with Detroit's community and political leaders.

If they had a gap in the meeting schedule, all of them would walk a neighborhood knocking on doors, seeking and often greeting possible voters.

One meeting Mike attended was in the town of Hamtramck. Congressman Lucian Nedzi arranged for Harold to talk with the wives of the city's firefighters and policemen. Their help was the key to winning the votes of that Polish community.

"You might remember, ladies," Lucian began, "Harold Ryan was my opponent in the last two elections. I am here to tell you that I would not have won those elections without your help.

"Now, I'm asking you to help my former opponent win a seat as Circuit Judge. I'm doing that for two reasons. First and foremost, he is a qualified lawyer who will do a good job as Circuit Judge. Second, it will get him out of my hair. He promised me that I won't have to face him in another primary election." The crowd of ladies erupted in cheers and laughter.

A lady in the crowd shouted. "He's not Polish. How can we trust his word on that?"

Over the laughter, Lillian Ryan shouted. "But you can take my word for it. He promised me, too. So, if he mentions the word Congress again, even in his sleep, I'd throw him out of the house." More cheers and laughter greeted her promise.

"She's not kidding." Harold told the crowd, "As Luician told you, you were the difference makers in his races against me. Now, you can be the difference makers in the Circuit Court race. My election will not only guarantee Lucian's seat in Congress free of serious challenge, but the Polish people of Hamtramck will have an Irish judge looking out for them." The ladies rose to their feet and applauded.

On the way out of the hall, Mike asked, "Is that the way it works in Detroit?"

Congressman Nedzi answered. "That's the way it works everywhere, young man, but especially in Detroit's ethnic neighborhoods. By the way, I'd like to read that report you and Harold did for my committee."

Nedzi was a member of the House Judiciary Committee.

"Congressman Conyers would skin me alive, sir," Mike reminded him, "He wanted to wait until after the election to consider releasing it to the committee."

"He's just doing Ford a favor by holding off, you know that, Mike. Let me read your copy. I won't release it to the press or anything."

"I didn't bring my copy with me, sir," Mike informed him. "But Harold has a copy. His job's not in jeopardy like mine."

"I'll ask him. But, you gotta know, Mike," Nedzi reminded him, "I'd never allow you to suffer if word about the report got out."

"Thank you, sir."

***

On election eve, Jim Killeen, his wife Georgia, Joe Yager and his wife Cathy, the Burkes, the Sullivans, and the Ryans met for supper at an eastside Chinese restaurant called the Golden Buddha.

"How is it that we have a free evening, ladies?" Harold asked with a sly look on his face. "The primary election is tomorrow, you know. Shouldn't we be working a neighborhood or attending a gathering of some sort?"

"Ya gotta slow down sometimes, Harold," Joe Yager reminded him, "Besides, we've done all we can.

"All day tomorrow, we've got you going around to the polling places thanking workers who will be passing out your literature. Lillian will be driven in another car by Alberta, doing the same thing in black neighborhoods. Mike will go with Lucian Nedzi to visit polling places in Polish neighborhoods. Prince will be driven by Gonzalee to polling places in black neighborhoods, too. So, relax, Harold. We've got everything covered."

"Just the same," Alberta announced. "Marilyn and I did it on purpose, don't ya' know. We wanted to close the office early, too, and take a break tonight."

"Do I sense a revolt in the ranks, ladies?"

"I don't think it's as serious as all that, Harold," Marilyn said. "After all, Lillian suggested it. She thought it would be good for all of your campaign staff to get together."

Jim Killeen, Harold's campaign manager, couldn't be left out of this conversation.

"Harold, cool your jets. We've got everything covered," he assured him.

Look at the menu, will ya'? The waitress is waiting for your order."

"Oh, my," he sighed. "It appears you've got me," he said. "I'll have the sweet n' sour shrimp, please."

SILVER SPRING

The morning after the election, Mike and Marilyn were on their way to Maryland. Harold had gotten the third most votes in all of Wayne County. He was a shoo-in to win a seat on the Circuit Court in November.

Michael was driving. "Did I tell you that Harold gave Nedzi his copy of our report?"

"No, you didn't," Marilyn said, surprised. "How in hell did that happen?"

"Lucian asked me for my copy, and I told him I didn't have it with me, but Harold had his. The two of them talked, and Harold agreed to let Lucian read his copy, but he wanted the Congressman to take him around to the west-side Polish churches. Remember all those Altar Society meetings we attended last week? Harold must have been the guest at thirty of them. That was part of the deal. Harold got into those gatherings, and Lucian got to read our report."

"Well, I'll be," Marilyn said. "Will Nedzi keep it to himself?"

"I'm not sure," Mike told his wife. "But, he's sort a' the Polish poster boy for the Democratic Party in Michigan. He often gets what he wants and often gets away with a lot of independent stuff, too. I wouldn't put it past him to bargain for something from Conyers in exchange for keeping it quiet. Then again, if Nedzi ran with the report and released it, Conyers would be off the hook with Ford. I suspect that's what will happen."

"We'll see," Marilyn said. "While we were in Michigan, I talked to Mary Woodward. Do you remember interviewing her in Dallas?"

"If I recall correctly, she and another lady were reporters for the Dallas Morning newspaper. They were standing on the Grassy Knoll when Kennedy was shot. Is that right?"

"That's the one."

"Why were you talking with her?"

"I thought I'd tempt her with the possibility of a peek at your report in exchange for a front-page headline in that newspaper she works for," Marilyn informed him.

"But, her editor declined on the grounds that the information was pirated and couldn't be verified. Mary put me in touch with another one of her colleagues who was with her on the Grassy Knoll, Ann Donald. It seems that Ms. Donald freelances with a weekly Dallas paper. The editor on that paper wasn't as squeamish. He'd love to run a story. If Conyers doesn't find a way to release the report, I'm thinking of sending Arnold a copy. It would give her a great exclusive, and she would get it plastered all over her newspaper in Dallas."

"A weekly? Who would ever see the damn thing?"

"I asked her that," Marilyn responded, "Arnold said that such a story would be picked up by the Associated Press and United Press International. That would spread it all over the country."

"Two things to remember, my dear," Mike told his wife. "First: releasing the report would ruin me in D.C. No one would hire me for anything there. Second: Ryan has to get elected. On top a' that," Mike continued, "We haven't talked about leaving Maryland and moving to Michigan, or did I miss that part?"

"Oops! Ya got me there, buddy." Marilyn admitted.

"As long as we're on the subject," Mike probed, "What about it?"

"I loved the people, Michael. The neighborhood around Wayburn was sort a' old. But, there was a real nice area a few blocks to the east and to the south of Outer Drive, and I loved Harper Woods."

"What did you think of the schools?"

"Everyone said that Stellwagon public school was top-notch. Jackie Sczymanski's a teacher there. Her husband Henry was running for the Circuit Court, too. She said it was the best elementary school in the city. But she wouldn't send her kids to the public middle school or to Finny High School. When Cathy Yager and I were passing out literature for Harold in Harper Woods, I saw some real nice homes for sale. St. Peter's Elementary School and Bishop Gallagher High School would be handy there, too. The principal at St. Peter's said to call him when we get settled. He thinks he'll have an opening on his Montessori preschool staff come January. Jackie would go to school there free."

"When did you get the time to do all this stuff? We were only there two weeks and you were working twelve-hour days on Harold's campaign, I thought."

"I did my job for Harold. But, there were a few things I had to check out, too."

"I guess you did," Mike agreed, "There is something else I need to run by you. If I took Harold's job offer, I'd be expected to do some politicking on a regular basis, ya know. How do you feel about that?"

"I fell in love with all that stuff, Michael. I'm surprised, but I really did. So, I wouldn't mind that at all, as long as I'd be involved, too."

"That wouldn't be a problem. You'd be a welcome worker on anyone's campaign. But, there may be another problem we haven't talked about." Mike continued.

"Oh, what's that?"

"There's another thing you need to know upfront," Mike continued, "Harold told me that, as his Court Clerk, I'd be expected to take a few classes at the University of Detroit Law School. The court will pay the tuition, but it will mean I'd have to spend an evening or two in class during the week and devote some study time to the course material at home."

"In for a penny, in for a pound, Michael," Marilyn responded with a sigh, "But, rather than just fool around with a course or two, you might as well get a law degree while you're at it,

"Harold is no spring chicken. He'll be gone from the bench after two terms, I figure," Marilyn continued, "You might as well set yourself up as an attorney on the Court's nickel while you're earning a paycheck."

Mike couldn't help laughing. "You do have everything worked out, don't you?" Mike remarked, "What other aspect of our lives have you decided?"

"I'm not sure, but you'll be the first to know. Right now, though, I do know what we'll be doing tonight after the kids are in bed."

"I can hardly wait," Mike said.

"Me too."

"Wait a minute. Not to leave the enticing thought of you in my arms tonight, but are you saying you wouldn't mind selling our Maryland house and moving to the Detroit area?"

Marilyn slid across the bench seat, closer to her husband. "Wouldn't you find it exciting, Michael?" Marilyn gushed. "We'd be starting a whole new life."

"Is that a yes?"

"That's absolutely a yes from me. How about you?"

"I'm all for it, too. Just you hold on to that report, though, until Harold wins his seat on the Circuit Court. OK? I don't want to be unemployed in Washington before I have another job. Also, I couldn't start until he's sworn in next January. We could move there the week after Christmas and be ready to go the first of the year. What do ya' think of that?"

"I like it. I met a neat gal, Janet Fikany," Marilyn told Mike, "Georgia Killeen introduced me to her. She and her husband, Jim, just opened a real estate office in Harper Woods. I'll call her and see if we can rent something in that community first. That'll give us a chance to look around. And, when we do find something, the girls will already be in St. Peters Elementary and near Bishop Gallagher High School."

"You've got this all figured out, don't you."

"Almost, except for the part when I tell my folks we're moving."

"There's that." Mike agreed.

AFTERWORD

It was early on December 27th, 1967, and the Burke family was on the road headed north to Michigan. They were followed by a moving van containing all their worldly goods.

The Burkes would spend that night at Joe and Cathy Yager's home in Detroit. Tomorrow morning Mike and Marilyn would meet the movers at their rental house on Dammen Street in Harper Woods.

Suddenly from the back seat, one of the kids asked a question.

"When we get to our new house," Jackie asked, "Can we have a dog?"

Marilyn immediately answered. "Wintertime is not the best time of the year to bring a little puppy into the house. That's more of a summertime thing, dear."

Quick to pick up on things, Ann asked. "Does that mean we can have a dog after winter is over?"

Mike knew his wife had left that door open; trouble for sure. He just smiled and decided to let her handle it.

"No, Ann," Marilyn stated firmly, "I didn't say that. All I meant is that we could discuss it after the winter is over."

But Susan was not about to let the matter die there. "What do you think we ought ta' call our dog, Jackie?" She asked her youngest sister.

"Barbie," Jackie responded. Her sisters laughed.

"What if it's a boy?" Ann asked.

"Ken, of course," Jackie said without hesitation. Her sisters had great fun with that, too. They laughed louder than they should and rolled around on the mattress in the back seat.

Marilyn just sighed. Mike could hardly keep from laughing aloud at her discomfort. The kids had often pulled this type of thing on him. He knew they would not drop the subject but would discuss it openly in front of their parents; and repeatedly.

These girls were so much like their mother. He could almost see himself walking a dog.

Mike had put a mattress and created a bed of sorts for them in the back seat. So, they could stretch out with pillows, blankets, and their Barbie stuff, of course.

Right now, they all dozed off.

"I have a surprise for you, Michael," Marilyn whispered.

Mike didn't have a clue what his wife had in store for him. "Be careful, sweetheart. I'm driving at almost 65 miles an hour with the kids in the back seat."

"In your dreams, Michael." Marilyn quipped.

She picked up an envelope from her stash of stuff on the floor of the front seat. Out of it, she pulled a newspaper dated December 20, 1967. She began to read it aloud to Mike.

"Warren Commission Covered Up JFK Killing

Exclusive for: The Real Truth by Ann Donald

This paper has recently come into the possession of a report prepared for the Judiciary Committee of the United States House of Representatives. While it was completed this past summer, it has yet to be made public. John Conyers, Democrat from Michigan and Chairman of the committee has refused to release this report and has declined to return our calls.

The findings of this exhaustive study are as follows:

There were shots fired at President Kennedy from the front as well as from the back of the motorcade on November 22, 1963.

There were more than three shots fired in the plot to kill President Kennedy on November 22, 1963.

Therefore, there was more than one assassin involved in the conspiracy to assassinate President Kennedy.

This study refutes the published findings in both the FBI report of December 1963 and the report of the Warren Commission of September 1964. Both of these reports insisted that there were only three shots fired, all from behind the president, and by only one man.

The Real Truth supports the recommendation of the editors of *Life Magazine* found in their issue of November 25, 1966. P.49

They concluded that the Warren Commission was flawed and incomplete. So, they recommended that an investigation of the assassination of John Fitzgerald Kennedy be reopened and conducted by an impartial body that has no connection to the government. (For the complete text of their recommendation, see page 3).

See our next issue for more details of the report and reactions."

Mike and Marilyn remained silent. The only sound they could hear was that of their car's tires on the highway.

"That's pretty straightforward," Mike finally commented," What do you think of it?"

"They didn't play loose with your report, did they, Michael? I hope the Associated Press picks it up. Just the same, Ann Donald promised to send me a copy of the paper whenever they ran more of your report."

"I'd like to be a mouse in Ford's office to hear his reaction. He should be screaming mad about now." Mike chuckled.

"No going back now, my dear."

"That's fine with me," Marilyn reminded him. "We're off on an adventure and a new life, Michael. I'm happy you're out of Washington."

Mike pulled his wife closer and drove with his right arm around her.

"Me too, sweetheart," Mike assured her, "As long as we're together."

REPORT ON THE ASSASSINATION
OF PRESIDENT JOHN KENNEDY

Prepared By:

Michael J. Burke

Harold Ryan

Page 2: The Charge of the House Judiciary Committee

In a 1966 Harris-Washington Post poll, sixty-seven percent of Americans said they did not believe the single shooter conclusion announced in both the FBI Report of December 1963 and the Warren Commission Report of September 1964.

In reaction, members of the House Judiciary Committee directed their chairman, Congressman John Conyers, and their minority leader, Congressman Gerald Ford, to initiate a study of the evidence surrounding the assassination of President John F. Kennedy.

The question the Committee wished answered first was: Did Oswald Act Alone?

To arrive at the answer to this question, investigators talked with persons involved in the post-assassination investigations and looked at other bodies of evidence collected for the FBI and Warren reports.

Page 3:

This report done for the Judiciary Committee deals with:

Directionality: did all the shots come from behind?

Shots: how many shots were fired?

Shooters: were all the shots fired by one assassin?

One section of this report will be devoted to each of the above questions. An appendix and notes dealing with the testimony taken will follow.

This will be followed by another section presenting conclusions and recommendations.

Page 4: Directionality

"The shots which killed President Kennedy and wounded Governor Connally were fired from the sixth-floor window at the southeast corner of the Texas Book Depository." *Warren Commission Report: Sep. 24, 1964.*

However:

"The physicians who attended President Kennedy in the Parkland Hospital ER identified his throat wound as one of entry." See Appendix A.

"Several physicians at Parkland and others at the scene of the assassination on Elm Street identified the head wound as one inflicted from the front." See Appendix B.

Shots from the front: The Grassy Knoll?

Ken O'Donnell: A Special Assistant to JFK, said. "I told the FBI what I had heard (two shots from behind the Grassy Knoll fence), but they said it couldn't have happened that way and that I must have been hearing things. So, I testified the way they wanted me to. I just didn't want to stir up more pain and trouble for the family. *Man of the House. By Thomas O'Neil Jr., p. 178*

Page 5

"As soon as I heard the shots, I turned toward the fence on the Grassy Knoll. Then, I got on the car phone and ordered, 'Move all available men out of my office to the railroad yard …and hold everything secure until homicide and other investigators should get there'. Dallas *Dallas County Sheriff J. E. Decker: Warren Commission Report Sep. 1964; Vol. 6, p. 287.*

Motorcycle Officer Bobby Hargis was positioned at the left rear of the presidential limo. A light breeze was blowing toward him.

"I had got splattered with blood (and) I was just back and left of Mrs. Kennedy..." *Warren Commission Report. Sep. 1964. Vol. 6, p. 247, 248.*

There were thirty-eight witnesses interviewed by Warren Commission investigators. All of them reported that one or more shots came from the direction of the Grassy Knoll and or suspicious activity in that area.

"In any event, no one present at the time saw anything at all suspicious." Congressman *Gerald Ford: Warren Commission Member. Life Magazine Oct. 2, 1964*

For more testimony, see Appendix C.

Page 6: How Many Shots Were Fired?

FBI Report: December 1963. "There were three shots fired. The first shot hit President Kennedy. The second shot hit Governor Connally. The third shot hit the president in the head."

While standing in front of the underpass, James Tague was hit in the face by a piece of cement. This incident was witnessed by Dallas County Deputy Sheriff Walthers and reported to the FBI the same day. The following summer, the FBI verified that a bullet had hit a curb and caused a cement fragment to hit Mr. Tague. *Warren Commission: Vol. 19. p. 502.*

Warren Commission Report: September 20, 1964. "The first shot missed; the second shot hit the president in the back at the base of his neck, exited, and then wounded Governor Connally. The third shot hit the president in the back of the head."

However, if we just listed the verified shots fired, the total number of shots exceeds those (three) announced in the FBI Report of Dec. 1963 and the Warren Commission Report of Sep. 1964.

Page 7: Verified Shots Fired

1. One shot hit President Kennedy in the back.

2. A separate shot hit the president in the throat.

3. Still another shot hit a street curb and wounded Mr. Tague on the cheek.

4. Another shot hit the president in the head.

5. A bullet was found by the physicians at Bethesda Hospital during the autopsy and given to Admiral Burkley, who was in the room. He then turned it over to FBI agents present (At Bethesda), who gave him a receipt for the bullet.

6. Another bullet fired was the one the FBI said hit Governor Connally.

7. One might also count the bullet found on a gurney at Parkland Hospital (the pristine bullet).

"The weight of the evidence indicates that there were three shots fired." *Warren Commission Report: Sep. 1964*

Author's Note: Even if one accepts the Warren Commission's "single bullet theory," it is clear that there were still at least four if not five shots fired, not just three.

Page 8

See Appendix D for more information.

Page 9: Were all the shots fired by one assassin?

"There is not one scintilla of proof that there was a conspiracy (more than one assassin), foreign or domestic..." *J. Edgar Hoover*

"The assassination of President Kennedy was the work of one man, Lee Harvey Oswald. There is no conspiracy, foreign or domestic." *New York Times: Sept. 27, 1964.*

Abraham Zapruder's film, taken from his position on the Grassy Knoll, clearly shows President Kennedy hit on the right front of his head. *Life Magazine: page 45, frame 6. Oct. 2, 1964*

"There is no evidence of a second man, or of other shots, or other guns." *Congressman Gerald Ford: Warren Commission member. Life Magazine, October 2, 1964*

Author's Note: If any of the shots were fired from the front or side of the president, there was more than one assassin at Dealey Plaza that November day. Should such be the case, therefore, the basis of both the FBI report and the Warren Commission report would be wrong.

See Appendix E for more information.

Page 10: Appendix A

Throat Wound: Front or Rear Entry?

Author's Note: If any of the shots were fired from the front of the president, there had to be more than one assassin in Dealey Plaza on November 22, 1963.

Dr. Perry: During an 11-22-63 afternoon press conference, he said the throat wound was one of entry. *New York Times November 23, 1963.* After an evening phone call from Secret Service Agent Elmer Moore on Nov. 22, 1963, Dr. Perry changed his story.

Dr. Crenshaw: Saw the throat wound and considered it one of entry. He was not interviewed by either the FBI or the Warren Commission investigators.

Dr. Carrico: Parkland ER physician. He saw the throat wound and considered it one of entry. He helped Dr. Perry perform the tracheotomy. *Warren Commission Testimony. Vol VI, page 478.*

Page 11

Dr. Kent Clark: Parkland ER physician: He saw a throat wound as an entry wound. *Warren Commission Deposition: Dallas, TX. March 21, 19645.*

Margaret Henchliffe: Parkland ER Nurse. She described Kennedy's throat wound: "It was just a little bullet hole in the middle of his neck...about as big as the end of my little finger...that looked like an entrance bullet hole..." *Warren Commission Deposition: Dallas, TX. March 21, 1964.*

Page 12: Appendix B

Head Wound: Bullet Exit in Front or Back?

Author's Note: both the FBI Report of December 1963 and the Warren Commission Report of September 1964 insisted that all the shots were fired from behind President Kennedy. There were witnesses who testified otherwise.

Dr. Kent Clark: He examined JFK at Parkland ER. He reported that the president was hit on the right front (occipital) with an exit wound in the back of the head. *Warren Commission Deposition: March 21, 1964.*

Dr. Perry: He examined JFK at Parkland ER. He said the president was hit on the right with an exit wound in back of the head. *Warren Commission Testimony: Vol. VI, p. 478.*

Dr. McClelland: Examined At Parkland ER. He testified that JFK was hit on the right with an exit wound in the back of his head. *Warren Commission Deposition: Dallas, TX. March 21, 1964.*

Page 13

Dr. Paul Peters: Examined President at Parkland ER. He saw a "...large defect in the right occipital area..." *Warren Commission Testimony. Vol. VI, p. 478.*

Clinton Hill: Saw head wound at back of JFK's head when protecting Mrs. Kennedy in the limo. *Secret Service Report: November 30, 1963*

Motorcycle Patrolman Bobby Hargis: Motorcycle and uniform was covered with blood & flesh. *Warren Commission Interview: Dallas, TX April 8, 1964.*

Gary & Gayle Newman: They saw a bullet hit JFK on the front right. *FBI Interview: Dallas, TX, November 24, 1963.*

Abraham Zapruder film: It clearly shows the bullet strike the president's head at the right front, the skull blown out and the head forced back.

Parkland Hospital ER Nurse Margaret Henchcliffe: She saw a large skull wound on the back of the president's head when she was cleaning his body before it was put into the bronze casket. *Warren Commission Deposition: Dallas, TX. March 21, 1964.*

Page 14

Secret Service Agent Roy Kellerman: He saw a large portion of the back of JFK's skull missing. *Warren Commission Report: Vol. 11, p 124.*

Secret Service Agent William Greer: He saw a portion of JFK's skull missing at the back right of Kennedy's head. *Warren Commission Testimony: Vol 11, page 124.*

Page 15: Appendix C

Were Any Shots Fired From the Grassy Knoll?

Author's Note: There were thirty-eight witnesses interviewed by the FBI and/or the Warren Commission investigators. All of them claimed to have heard one or more shots coming from the Grassy Knoll area. None of these claims were considered credible enough to investigate further. The following is a sample of those thirty-eight witnesses. For a complete list, Google Grassy Knoll Witnesses: The JFK Assassination.

Sheriff Decker: Sent his deputies to secure RR and parking area behind the Grassy Knoll area. *Warren Commission Deposition: Dallas, TX. April 16, 1964*

Dallas Chief of Police Curry: Looked to Grassy Knoll upon hearing the first shot.

Bill and Gayle Newman Watched from Grassy Knoll. Bill Newman testified to the FBI that shots came from behind them. *FBI Interview: Dallas, TX. November 24, 1963.*

Seymour Weitzman: Deputy Sheriff. Went to the Grassy Knoll to investigate and was sent away by men showing

Page 16

Secret Service identifications. Warren Commission Deposition: April 1, 1964.

Sam Holland: Union Terminal Co. supervisor. He stood with his son by Triple Underpass. He heard four shots and saw a puff of smoke on the Grassy Knoll. *Warren Commission Testimony: Dallas, TX. April 8, 1964, 2:20 PM*

Mary Woodward: She was a reporter for the Dallas Morning News. Watched the motorcade from Grassy Knoll. She believed that shots came from behind her. *FBI Interview: Dallas, TX. December 6, 1963.*

Maggie Brown: She was a reporter for Dallas Morning News. Watched the motorcade from the Grassy Knoll. She believed that shots came from behind her. *FBI Interview: Dallas, TX. December 6, 1963.*

Ken O'Donnell: Presidential Aide. In motorcade. Believed shots came from Grassy Knoll. *'Man of the House,' by Thomas O'Neil Jr. p. 178.*

Senator Ralph Yarborough: He was in the motorcade car with Vice President Johnson. An experienced hunter, he told reporters after the assassination, "...you could smell the gunpowder." *James M. Perry: Reporter for the National Observer in Dallas traveling with the press corps on Nov. 22, 1963.*

Page 17

Mrs. Elizabeth Cabell: Wife of Dallas mayor. She rode in the motorcade. She smelled gun smoke coming from the Grassy Knoll. *Warren Commission Deposition: Dallas, TX. February 13, 1964.*

Forrest Sorrels: Secret Service: In motorcade's lead car. Testified he thought shots came from the Grassy Knoll. *Warren Commission Deposition: May 7, 1964.*

Dallas patrolman Joe Marshall Smith: Ran to the fence on the Grassy Knoll after the shots. He was told to leave by a man who claimed to be a Secret Service Agent. *Warren Commission Deposition: Dallas, TX. July 23, 1964.*

Page 18: Appendix D

Were All the Shots Fired by One Assassin?

Author's Note: If even one of the president's wounds was inflicted from the front, all the shots could not have been fired from the rear of the motorcade. Therefore, there had to be multiple assassins.

Dr. Kent Clark: Parkland ER said the head wound was inflicted on the front right of JFK's head and exited on the back. *Warren Commission Deposition: Dallas, TX. March 21, 1964.*

Dr. McClelland: Parkland ER doctor said JFK's skull opening indicated a bullet hit on the front of his head, exiting on the back of the skull. *Warren Commission: Dallas, TX. March 21, 1964.*

DPD Sgt. D.V. Harkness: "I saw a group of men at the fence on the Grassy Knoll. I was told to leave by a man who said they were Secret Service." *Warren Commission Deposition: Dallas, TX. April 9, 1964.*

Bill and Gayle Newman: Watched from Grassy Knoll. They told the FBI that they saw JFK hit in the head from the front.

Page 19

And they believed that the shot was fired from behind them. *FBI Interview: Dallas, TX. November 24, 1963.*

M. Henchcliffe: Parkland ER Nurse. She saw the president's large head wound on the back of his head when cleaning JFK's body prior to its transfer into the bronze casket. *Warren Commission Deposition: Dallas, TX. March 21, 1964.*

Dr. Perry: Parkland ER described the wound on the head as a rear exit wound. *Warren Commission Testimony: Dallas, TX. Vol VI p. 478.*

Sam Holland: Stood on the railroad bridge known as the triple underpass at the west end of Dealey Plaza. "I counted four shots..." *Warren Commission: Vol. 6 p243. April 8, 1964*

Mary Woodward: Journalist for *Dallas Morning News*. She wrote for her paper on 23 Nov. 1963. "Suddenly, there was a horrible, ear-shattering noise coming from behind us and a little to the right." *Warren Commission Exhibit No 2084, Vol. 24. p. 520.*

Maggie Brown: Reporter for *Dallas Morning News*. She stood on the Grassy Knoll. She believed the bullets were fired from behind her. *FBI Interview: Dallas, TX. December 6, 1963.*

Page 20

DPD Patrolman Joe Marshall Smith: Headed toward the fence on the Grassy Knoll. He was told to leave by a man who claimed to be Secret Service. *Warren Commission Deposition: Dallas, TX. July 7, 1964.*

Page 21: Appendix E

Were all the shots fired by one assassin?

Frazier, Robert A. FBI Special Agent assigned to the FBI Crime Laboratory in Washington D.C. He testified that it took him (His best time out of three tries) 4.6 seconds to hit a target 3 times, 100 yards away with Oswald's Mannlicher-Carcano rifle. *Warren Commission Testimony: Vol iii. p. 407.*

In response to a direct question, he said he would have to add an additional second per shot if he was firing at a moving target. (a total of 6.6 seconds). *Warren Commission. Vol. iii, p. 407.*

Ronald Simmons: Chief of the Infantry Weapons Evaluation Branch of the Ballistics Research Laboratory of the Dept. of the Army.

Recruited three riflemen considered 'expert' by the National Rifle Association. They Fired 21 shots each at three stationary targets. Only one of the 'experts' hit the target within the WC's time limit of 5.15 seconds. *Warren Commission. Vol. iii, p. 446.*

Page 22: Findings

This investigation has led us to believe that there is substantial evidence that:

There were more than three shots fired in the plot to kill President Kennedy on November 22, 1963.

There were shots fired at President Kennedy from the front as well as from behind.

There was more than one assassin involved in the killing of President Kennedy on November 22, 1963.

Page 23: Recommendation

Therefore, we recommend the House Judiciary Committee support the action suggested in the *Life Magazine* editorial published on November 25, 1966.

"One conclusion is inescapable: the national interest deserves clear resolution of the doubts. A new investigating body should be set up, perhaps at the initiative of Congress. In a scrupulously objective and unhurried atmosphere, without the pressure to give the assurance to a shocked country, it should re-examine the evidence and consider other evidence the Warren Commission failed to evaluate." *Life Magazine. November 25, 1966. p. 49b.*

BIBLIOGRAPHY

Mafia Kingfish: Carlos Marcello and the Assassination of John F. Kennedy. Author: John H. Davis. McGraw Hill 1989

LBJ and the Conspiracy to Kill Kennedy: A Coalescence of Interests. Author: Joseph P. Farrell. Adventures Unlimited Press. 2011

Breach of Trust: How the Warren Commission Failed the Nation and Why. Author: Gerald D. McKnight, 2013

Rush to Judgment. Author: Mark Land. A Fawcett Crest Book. 1966

Assassination Science. Ed. James H. Fetzer. Cat Feet Press. 1998

A Cruel and Shocking Act: The Secret History of the Kennedy Assassination. Author: Philip Shenon. Henry Hold and Co. 2003

JFK Has Been Shot: A Parkland Hospital Surgeon Speaks Out. Author: Charles A. Crenshaw MD. Pinnacle Books 1992

The JFK Assassination Diary. Author: Edward Jay Epstein. 2013

The Bureau: My Thirty Years in Hoover's FBI. Author: William Sullivan. W.W. Norton. 1979

CIA Rogues and the Killing of the Kennedys: How and Why US Agents Conspired to Assassinate JFK and RFK. Author: Patrick Nolan. Skyhorse Publishing. 2013

The Man Who Killed Kennedy: The Case Against LBJ. Author: Robert Stone. Skyhorse Publishing 2013

Best Evidence: Disguise and Deception in the Assassination of John F. Kennedy. Author: David S. Lifton. Macmillan Publishing.1980

The Kennedy Detail. Author: Gerald Blaine. Gallery Books. 2010

Crossfire: The Plot That Killed Kennedy. Author Jim Marris. Basic Books. 2013

Trauma Room One: The JFK Medical Cover-Up Exposed. Author: Charles A. Crenshaw, M.D. Paraview Press 2001

Not in Your Lifetime: Fifty Years on, Weighing the Evidence. Author: Anthony Summers. Open Road Press. 1980

The Advance Man: An Off-beat Look at What Really Happens in Political Campaigns. Authors: Jerry Bruno and Jeff Greenfield. Bantam Books1972

Kennedy and Johnson. Author: Evelyn Lincoln. Holt, Rinehart and Winston. 1968.

The Warren Commission Report: Report of the President's Commission on the Assassination of President John F. Kennedy. Barnes and Noble Books. 1964

Last Word: My indictment of the CIA in the Murder of JFK. Author: Mark Lane. A Herman Graff Book. 2012

Plausible Denial: Was the CIA Involved in the Assassination of JFK? Author: Mark Lane. A Herman Graff Book. 1991.

Who's Who in the JFK Assassination: An A-to-Z Encyclopedia. Author: Michael Benson. A Citadel Press Book.1993.

Conscience of a Conspiracy Theorist. Author: Robert Lockwood Mills. Algora Publishing. 2011

E-Books

Coup d' Etat. Author: Jerry Knoth

The Park Near the Underpass. Author: James Charles Schulz

JFK Assassination – 50 Years (On 60 Minutes). Author: Dr. Frey Hardy

Killing JFK: 50 Years, 50 Lies. Author: Dr. Lance Moore

Master Chronology of JFK Assassination. Author: Walt Brown Ph.D.

LBJ: The Mastermind of the JFK Assassination. Author: Phillip F. Nelson

The Complete Guide to the 1963 JFK Assassination. Progressive Management Publication.

Survivors Guild: The Secret Service Failure to Protect President Kennedy. Author: Vincent Michael Palmara. 2013

Magazines

Life Magazine Issues: November 1963 (Special Issue); November 29, 1963; December 6, 1963; November 25, 1966; October 4, 1964.

Time Magazine: November 25, 2013

The Day Kennedy Died: Time Home Entertainment 2013

ABOUT THE AUTHORS

Michael J. Deeb was born and raised in Grand Rapids, Michigan. His undergraduate and graduate education centered on American studies. His doctorate was in management. He was an educator for nineteen years, most of which saw him teaching American history and historical research.

His personal life found him as a pre-teen spending time regularly at the public library, reading non-fiction works of history. This passion has continued to this day. Teaching at the college, university, and high school levels only increased his passion for such reading and research.

Since 2005, he and his wife have lived in Sun City Center, Florida. In the fall of 2007, he published the first historical novel in the Drieborg Chronicles series, *Duty and Honor*. The sequel, *Duty Accomplished*, was completed in 2008. *Honor Restored* followed in 2009, and the Lincoln Assassination became available in 2010. He wrote and published a prequel, 1860, to this trilogy in 2011 and concluded the series with, *The Way West* in 2013.

Currently, Dr. Deeb is working as a Civil War speaker on the ships of the American Cruise Lines.

Robert Lockwood Mills spent most of his life as a Wall Street broker and as an instructor in financial planning for Adelphi University. In middle age, he began to focus on historical research; beginning in 1994, he has authored eight published non-fiction books, including, *It Didn't Happen the Way You Think* (Heritage Books 1994), *The Illustrated History of Stamford (CT)* (American Historical Press, 2002), *The Lindbergh Syndrome: Heroes and Celebrities in a New Gilded Age* (Wheatmark, 2005), and most recently *Conscience of a Conspiracy Theorist* (Algora Publishing, 2011), which studied the Kennedy assassination with an emphasis on governmental and media efforts to stigmatize honest skeptics as conspiracy theorists.

Other works consist of six stage plays, two personal biographies, a baseball book (written entirely from memory), and a history of the Darien (CT) Country Club. Mills also authored a docudrama, "The Trial of John Wilkes Booth," which was broadcast by Connecticut Public Radio in 1999.

Mills has been Project Editor for five Reader's Digest Illustrated Trade Books on historical topics and now does free-lance editing work for local authors. His diverse interests include acting and directing, choral singing, songwriting, satire, and crossword puzzle construction. He is a widower with three grown daughters and four grandchildren and lives in Florida with his companion and fellow author, Rosemary Clifton.

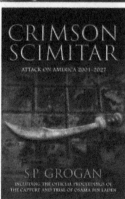